ESPECIALLY FOR GIRLS™
presents

He Noticed
I'm Alive . . .
and Other
Hopeful Signs

a novel by
MARJORIE SHARMAT

Delacorte Press / New York

for my sister Rosalind Weinman

and her beautiful portraits

Published by
Delacorte Press
1 Dag Hammarskjold Plaza
New York, N.Y. 10017

Manufactured in the United States of America

First printing

Library of Congress Cataloging in Publication Data
Sharmat, Majorie Weinman.
He noticed I'm alive—and other hopeful signs.
Summary: Jody's fifteenth summer brings major changes in her father's
love life and her own, when she becomes attracted to his lady's friend's
son.
[1. Single-parent family—Fiction] I. Title.
PZ7.S5299He 1984 [Fic]
ISBN 0-385-29351-8
Library of Congress Catalog Card Number: 84-4329

This book is a presentation of
Especially for Girls™
Weekly Reader Books.

Weekly Reader Books offers book clubs for children from
preschool through high school.

For further information write to:
Weekly Reader Books
4343 Equity Drive
Columbus, Ohio 43228

Especially for Girls™
is a trademark of Weekly Reader Books.

Edited for Weekly Reader Books
and published by arrangement with
Delacorte Press.

Chapter 1

My life changed in four hours. This is not unusual. A life can change in four seconds. A split second. Three new people came into my life in those four hours. One was Mrs. Opal Spiegel. The others were Gossamer Green and her son, Matt. I would like to mention Matt Green first, but I have to be chronological about this.

I'm Jody Kline, I'm fifteen, and I live with my father, Gerald, in a house that was expensive even before all houses got to be expensive. We have a four-times-a-week maid, Betty.

I also have a mother who's not around. Two years ago she left a note, friendly and exuberant and vague, addressed to "Gerald and Jody dears," and signed "Love always," and she split. She wrote something in the note about needing to find herself, which is a popular expression I don't understand. In the two years she's been gone, there have been friendly and exuberant and vague notes and cards from all over the world, signed "Love always." It's as if my mother were simply an inveterate traveler conscientiously reporting on her travels.

My father really isn't interested in being married to an inveterate traveler and note writer. He's been trying to get a divorce. It's not easy, because my mother hasn't been available for consultation or whatever you're supposed to be available for when somebody's trying to divorce you. Still, my father has been making headway. He's a lawyer and he knows lots of angles.

I felt sad and abandoned when my mother left. But there was something so crazy and so flighty about what she did that it seemed more like a bad joke than a major tragedy. My father was practical about the whole thing. He hired Betty for four days instead of her usual two, and he worked harder at his law office, and he started to date. He filled up his life.

I have school and friends, including my best friend, Alison August. Some of my friends are boys, but they're not what I would call boyfriends. None of them ever appealed to me that way. I knew why when I met Matt Green. He appealed to me instantly, the moment he walked into my house. He walked *right* into my house. How's that for service?

My life-changing four hours happened nearly three months ago. Every once in a while I help my father when he has to entertain. I guess I'm the hostess, which makes me sound about forty years old and as if I'm walking around in a sweeping gown. It's a drag, but it doesn't happen often enough for me to complain.

Summer vacation from school had just begun. I was free all day, free to cook for the dinner guests my father had invited to our house. Betty does most of our cooking, but it was one of her days off. I like to cook sometimes, especially in French. I have eight French cookbooks. But I hate having strangers for dinner. Especially my father's friends. They act so congenial and civilized, so I have to be too. Offering food, the use of my house, the ashtrays (I don't really mean it, the Surgeon General has determined that cigarette smoking is dangerous to your health, don't you old folks *read?*), the bathrooms, the brand-new, thick, velvet, pucker-free guest towels with the surrealistic appliquéd butterflies, and 100 percent of my conversational self is too much. Having strangers for dinner is an evening of relentless *up*.

My father had told me that the guests' names were Gossamer and Matt Green, so I assumed they were a married couple, possibly with a couple of kids whose superior intelligence they could brag about. My father specializes in highly intelligent friends. Lawyers like to do that.

I was late in starting my *noix de veau à la chartreuse* because I got involved in watching an old Bette Davis movie on TV. I had all my ingredients together and was about to start cooking when the doorbell rang.

I muttered my favorite word, "Rats!" I told myself I didn't have to answer. Alison never answers doorbells when her parents take trips and leave her alone. Alison's house becomes an insurmountable fortress, the doorstep littered with newspapers, packages from parcel post, free samples, circulars, and curdled milk. When the mood hits her, she steps out and collects these things. She has never been robbed, but her house has frequently been tinkered with by cruising break-in hopefuls who were positive that it was unoccupied.

The doorbell rang again. And again. Three times was impolite. Pushy.

I'm intimidated by pushy people, and a two-and-one-half-inch-thick door was an insufficient psychological barrier between me and this gale-force personality that was trying to reach me.

I walked to the door and opened it. The first of the three people who were going to change my life was standing there.

Chapter 2

She was a well-dressed woman and her hand was poised to ring again. A suburban-type lady, aggressively clean, and smelling of bottled carnations, she was carrying a sheaf of papers that could only mean she was door-to-door and wanted some of my time.

"Good afternoon," she said, and smiled. "If you have a few moments, I'd like to ask your opinion about a product. *I am not selling anything.*"

I would have laughed, but I don't think it's smart to laugh in front of pushy people, even if they aren't armed or capable of brute strength. The woman was selling her way into my house. She was charm and graciousness and all smiles, confident that she was a thousand light-years away from a snake-oil salesman, when in fact she was his certifiable disciple.

"How many questions do you have?"

"Just a few. This is a quality product. We visit only select households, and therefore any answers *you* could give me would be particularly valuable."

"I'm expecting company for dinner, so I don't have much time."

"I understand," said the woman.

I knew the woman didn't believe me. People were probably always giving her excuses. I'm busy—I don't want any—I gave at the office—Come back later—I have a sick mother inside—The sprinkler system is about to go on and it reaches the very spot where you're standing—I have a vicious dog.

"I'm really having company tonight."

"Fine. Then is your mother home, dear?"

"No."

The woman stood and looked at me. I looked at her. When she wasn't making a pitch, she was attractive. The longer she stood silently, the more attractive she became. Suddenly I opened the door wider and invited her in. I don't know why. Maybe I was thinking about all the doors closing on her, rejection after rejection.

She stepped inside, bringing waves of carnations with her. Her mood changed. She was gathering power. "Well, I must say you've got better manners than that little snip across the street. She let me stand in her doorway for half an hour asking her questions. Who does she think she is? Just because she's got a big house. I had a beautiful home in Scarsdale for six years. Beautiful home. Custom built. Plaster walls. May I sit here?"

Half an hour! How many questions did she have? I was afraid to ask again.

She sat down in the gold-on-gold striped velvet easy chair without waiting for an answer. I didn't want her to sit there. It was a soft, comfortable, enveloping, almost sensuous chair that embraced its occupants like an eager lover. That was my father's description of the chair. The lady's sitting there could cost me at least fifteen minutes more than if she had got into the stiff, high-backed, and slightly scratchy blue job that was, in addition, located directly under an arthritic blast of cold air from the air-conditioning vent.

She was looking at the room, first turning her head from side to side, and then nodding up and down, as if she were doing those exercises that promise a firmer, lovelier chin in only two weeks. "Your home is charming," she said. "One can always tell when a great deal of love has gone into furnishing a home. It shows immediately."

She opened her very large, squashy pocketbook. "My arsenal," she said, and she smiled again.

Good. She was down to business.

She pulled out as purple and orange and blue aerosol can and held it high as if it were winner and still champion. "This," she said with pride, "is a product so new that one almost feels like whispering about it in hushed tones."

I nodded. "I guess you want to ask me a question about it. Go right ahead." *Out the door,* I felt like adding. I wanted her to leave. But I tried to be polite.

"Well, this product is, would you believe it, **a deodor-ant!**"

"Yes, I believe it. Is that the first question?"

"Heavens, no. Now, as you see, there is a young lady pictured on the can, and she is pale blue. My first question is, Do you find the can aesthetically pleasing?"

"Yes."

"And?"

"And what?"

"What we're looking for is an in-depth answer. Why do you find it pleasing?"

"Well, the girl, being blue, looks cool, so my reaction is that I could be cool if I used the product."

"What about the orange and purple?"

"Well, the orange looks hot, but the purple looks cool, and, as I said, the blue girl looks cool, so I would answer, *in depth*, that the can is saying that if you're hot you can get to be cool by using the product, and I think it's very clever, and I really couldn't say another word about the can."

The woman was scribbling away, saying "cool," "hot," and mumbling to herself. Finally she looked up. "Excellent," she said. She pulled something else from her arsenal. It was another can, identical to the first except that it was pink and green with a pale orange girl.

"Now," she said, "do you find this color combination more pleasing or less pleasing than the first?"

"I find it the same."

"But, my dear, how can it be the same when it's different?"

"Okay, it's vile."

"In depth, please."

I stood up. "I'd really like to help you, but I've got company coming. Your first can was definitely aesthetically pleasing, and I'll buy it when it comes out if you'll give me the name."

"I'm not selling anything, remember? You're really a marvelous interviewee. This will take just a bit longer. Could I trouble you for a glass of water, please?"

I went into the kitchen and took a pitcher of iced coffee from the refrigerator. I poured some into a glass and took it to the woman.

"Why, iced coffee," she exclaimed, as if she hadn't expected anything more than water. But I knew she had.

It was my farewell gift. "Could you come back tomorrow? I'll have more time then."

The woman moved the glass of coffee in a small circular motion so that the ice tinkled. I had seen this done much better in the old Bette Davis movie I had just watched. "Coming back never works," she said as she started to sip her coffee. "They say tomorrow, and I come back, and they don't answer the bell."

She looked down into her arsenal, which I suddenly noticed was bulging. Was there a gun in it? I had let her into the house and she was a stranger.

"I can't understand why anyone would shoot her," the neighbors would say. "She had no enemies, and she got all *A*'s at school. However, I don't think she was a regular churchgoer."

The woman took a handkerchief from her arsenal and wiped her mouth. I had forgotten to give her a napkin. "I'm a widow," she said. "A door-to-door widow. Do you know what that means? I don't count. I'm someone whom most people are never going to see again. My husband said something many years ago and I never forgot it. He said the measure of a good person is how they act toward someone they're never going to see again. Now, I have only two more cans to show you, and then there are just five fragrance questions, three size questions, three brand-name questions, and four competitor-comparison questions, and we're all through."

I gave up. I'm only fifteen, and this lady was experienced. If I didn't answer her questions, I was a rat. How did it come to this? She sat there with her spray-can weapons. Spray-and-Play was the projected name, and what did I think of that? In depth, please.

At last she got to the final category, which was What is your annual income? Is it under 5,000 dollars, between 5,000 and 10,000 dollars, or 10,000 and 20,000 dollars, or 20,000 and 30,000 dollars, or over 30,000 dollars?

"Well, you're obviously too young to work," she said, "so how about your mother and father?"

"My mother is . . . my mother is a travel agent. But she just does it for fun. And my father is unemployed."

I'm not a liar, so why did I lie?

"Oh, I'm terribly sorry," the woman said. "How can you afford this house?"

"Is that in the questionnaire?"

She looked up sharply. "Well, I usually don't ask questions of the unemployed."

"But you knew that *I* don't work."

Why was I pursuing this when all I really wanted was to get this woman out of the house?

"I thought you *belonged* to the employed," she said. "That would make your opinions legitimate." She stood up and, carefully clutching her arsenal and papers, walked slowly toward the door. She stopped. She stopped! What now? Would she be here forever? She was admiring a painting near the door. "What a beautifully executed painting," she said. "It's from Spain, isn't it?"

"Yes. How did you know?"

"I lived in Spain for four years. After my husband died."

"You did?" She had lived in *Spain?* I couldn't picture her beyond a suburban neighborhood. She seemed so caught up in what she was doing that it seemed impossible that she had ever had any other kind of life. "What were you doing in Spain?"

Now *I* was asking the questions.

"I had a boyfriend there. He was a painter. He painted scenes like this one, but with more passion and drama. He was very successful. It was an idyllic life while it lasted."

"What happened?"

"He found someone he liked better than me. Painters can be emotional and unstable, you know. It's part of their charm and part of their tragedy."

The woman looked wistful. When she stopped asking questions, she turned into somebody else. Maybe she turned into her real self. It was amazing. She had been part of a grand love affair in Spain.

"So what did you do?"

"I returned to the States. I had to make a living, and here I am. I do this because I have to do it. I'm part of the American free enterprise system. I push. I shove. I'm strong. I'm overwhelming. But I get my foot in the door. I survive. I hope you'll never have to survive. But if you do, you'll know what I mean."

I already knew what she meant. I wanted to ask her more questions. She had become interesting. This was crazy. I was late in getting ready for the Greens, and now I was making myself even more late.

But she was through. She opened the door. The warm air transformed her back into her outdoors self, the Scarsdale alumna, ringer of doorbells, carrier of carnation scents. She paused. "By the way, my name is Mrs. Spiegel, and it's been a pleasure meeting you." Her voice was kind and sincere. "I do hope that your father finds employment soon."

I nodded. I had scored a small, pointless, and cowardly victory. Mrs. Spiegel's husband would have thought I was a rotten human being. I never expected to see her again.

I watched her while she went down my front steps and walked up the street. I tried to imagine her entertaining in her beautiful home in Scarsdale, or sitting on a beach in Spain with the wind blowing through her hair while she watched her boyfriend paint. Now here she was, rebuilding her life by ringing doorbells. She really was a survivor. Even though she had forced herself on me, even though she had wasted my time, I admired her. Good luck and good fortune, Mrs. Spiegel.

I went back to the kitchen to work on the meal. And to the dining room to check on the table setting. And to the bathroom to replace slivers with new soap. My father always says that the better the house, the less likely that guests will expect to see evidence of how the host and hostess live on an everyday basis. They don't expect to see a robe hanging from a bathroom hook, underwear drying in the shower, plastic bags of moth-flaked clothes brushing against their coats in the front closet, or bottles of vitamin pills, pieces of mail, loose trading stamps, and bills on a kitchen counter.

Four hours after I opened the door for Mrs. Spiegel, the front door opened again. I heard my father calling, "Jody, we're here."

My father was standing just outside the open door. A woman was standing beside him. In an instant I got the feeling that she was going to be the replacement for my mother. It just flashed through my head. But how could that be, when she came with her husband, Matt? There was a man standing in the dark behind her, like an afterthought. What a way to treat your husband! Then the three of them walked into the house.

I stared at Matt Green. He wasn't anybody's husband. He looked about eighteen or nineteen, handsome, the kind of guy you sometimes see at a distance but know you'll never be lucky enough to meet.

"Jody," my father said, "I'd like you to meet Gossamer Green and her son, Matt."

Matt extended his hand. I hope I didn't *grab* it.

Chapter 3

We were sitting at the dinner table. My meal turned out fine, but it felt strange sharing it with the bronzed god and goddess my father had imported from New York City. Gossamer and Matt both had suntans. He looked as if he had got his outside. She looked as if she had got hers on purpose. And where did she get her stupid name? I imagined that people always asked her about her name, so I didn't. They probably told her it was lovely. Gossamer had blond hair that had been carefully done to look as if it hadn't been done. She looked like a professional at finding exactly the right clothes, the right accessories, the right trappings and props for her life. She reminded me of some of the very rich kids at school who always have plenty of money to spend or, as Alison had put it, who have "this really gross instinct for keeping the economy moving."

Still, that wasn't a reason not to like her. Well, how about this? She had the same first initial as my father. I have a quirky prejudice against couples who have the same first initial. It's as if they've been prepackaged, computerized to match. They're Jack and Jill smugly going up the hill together in shrink-wrap.

Why was I thinking of Gossamer and my father as a *couple?* It wasn't only the way they looked together. From their conversation I realized that they had been going out together a lot. Why hadn't my father told me about her? My father often works late and gets home after midnight, so when he's not home in the evening, I don't give it a second thought. Now it was dawning on me that this might be a significant family-type dinner. Maybe I was meeting my future stepmother and stepbrother.

My future stepbrother, if that's what he was, was tall and assured. He looked as if he never got a headache, never made a wrong turn on a highway, and actually wanted the magazines he subscribed to. He was also very quiet. He had hardly said a word all night. Maybe he resented my father for taking out his mother. His parents were divorced. I figured that out when Gossamer referred to her ex-husband every five minutes.

I knew I was supposed to make conversation, but I didn't know what kind of conversation to make. I was the official hostess. I was supposed to keep the show on the road. I don't consider myself to be a good talker. Some kids think I'm kind of mystically quiet. My best thoughts seem to exist inside myself and thrive on isolation. When I expose them to the light of the outside world, they become dreary and discolored like a peeled potato. I keep this peeled-potato theory to myself.

"Are you planning to go to college?"

Matt was asking me a question. It surprised me. It was

so direct, and he asked it suddenly, without any connection to anything that had gone before. We had all been eating dessert silently.

He was staring at me. He was sitting across the table from me, but during most of the dinner I could have been an empty chair or an extension of our seascape wallpaper.

My father answered the question. "She's hoping for Yale."

I glared at my father. Why couldn't *I* answer the question!

I looked at Matt. "Well, I'm thinking about Yale, but I'm also thinking about art school. I don't have to decide yet. I'm only starting my junior year this September. I don't know if I'd get accepted at Yale anyway, even though Dad—"

"Now, Jody, with your marks and my being an alum—"

"But I'm not sure about wanting . . ."

My voice trailed off. My father and I were having another of our unfinished dialogues, interrupting each other like TV news announcers, each with an incoming bulletin more timely and important than the last.

I love my father. But I wish he weren't so, well, *upper class.* You can tell he is just by looking at him. Just one quick glance and you'd know that he is not a fan of subways, delicatessens, potboiler movies, or bowling alleys. You would connect him to vanishing-breed tailors with pins in their mouths, dining places with pure linen tablecloths and napkins, engraved scratch pads, taxis and limousines, season tickets to the opera, and private clubs with three- or four-figure membership fees.

I was out of words. My father turned to Matt and said, "Art is a little hobby with Jody."

I found some words. "No, it isn't," I said. "It's major."

"There seems to be a difference of opinion here," Matt said, looking first at me and then at my father.

"Nothing that a few conversations can't turn into an all-out war," said Gossamer. She gave my father a kind of knowing-parent look, as if she was his ally.

I was ready to change the subject. But Matt pressed on. "What do you *really* want to do, Jody?"

I realized that he wasn't honoring the rules of the game of dinner guest. Superficial is the name. If the subject matter gets too close to home, switch.

Gossamer put her hand on my father's arm. "Gerald, she just wants to fulfill herself. All the kids do."

"I don't think of it that way," I said. "I love to draw and paint, and I might want to try to make a career out of it. Give it a chance, you know."

"Gerald, she just wants to get her feet a teensy-weensy bit wet," said Gossamer the translator.

Teensy-weensy? I rolled my eyes toward the ceiling.

"Could we see some of your work?" asked Matt.

I was beginning to feel complimented by his interest. When did he want to see my work? Now? At a later time, when we were alone? I liked the idea of a later time. It meant I would see him again. I fished in my head for an answer. But Gossamer came up first. "Let's put it on hold. I'm dying for some coffee. What do I have to do to get some?"

I stood up. I had forgotten to make coffee. I went to the kitchen.

Gossamer and my father monopolized the conversation for the rest of the evening. Gossamer told us about friends who had been robbed in broad daylight. "I thought it was happening to me the other day at Altman's," she said. "The woman next to me looked so menacing. But she was only trying to return a hot comb." They also talked about the best place to buy imported wines. I tried not to yawn.

Matt and I exchanged glances, but I wouldn't call them meaningful glances. They were just glances. I wanted to ask him questions about himself. I knew he was going to be a college freshman, because his mother had mentioned it. I knew he was planning to be a lawyer, because his mother had mentioned it. Finally I knew it was time for them to go home, because his mother had mentioned it.

I enjoy watching adults say good night. It's usually so gushy. But maybe the enthusiasm is genuine because they're so happy about leaving one another. Unfortunately my father told Gossamer he'd call her the next day.

I felt like saying "Good-bye forever" to Matt, as if to remind him that he might not see me again if he didn't try to. He said, "It was nice meeting you," which unfortunately is high on my list of nothing expressions. I wondered if he'd ever call me or pursue the art thing.

I didn't have a clue.

Chapter 4

I called Alison right after the Greens left. It was past midnight, but that didn't matter. I don't know when Alison and her family sleep, but kids are allowed to phone Alison anytime they want. This makes her popular at school, because the word got around that Alison's family doesn't have any rules at all, and how did she manage *that?* My father said that the family simply doesn't sleep, and their body metabolism badly needs checking.

"The Greens just left," I said.

"The Greens? Oh, the Greens, your father's friends. What were they like? No, let me guess. They were two slightly wizened creatures dressed in green jumpsuits with flashing antennae on their heads. They pulled up to your house in an equally green Avis rent-a-spaceship. 'We're the Greens from outer space,' they said, 'and we were told not to miss your tasty *noix de veau à la chartreuse* while we're on Earth.' "

"Alison!"

"Don't stop me. I'm hot. 'Come in,' you said. 'Sit

down, take off your antennae, and make yourselves comfortable. I hope you don't smoke.'

" 'We'd like to wash up first, if you don't mind,' said the creatures.

" 'Sure,' you said. 'Help yourselves to my brand-new, thick, velvet, pucker-free guest towels with the surrealistic appliquéd butterflies.' "

"Alison, stop it! Matt Green is about eighteen and he's out of this world."

"See, I was right. What have I just been telling you? Out of this world."

"My father's been dating his mother."

"I don't get it. Were they trying to match this guy up with you? And if so, did it work?"

"Hold on. My father's been taking out this woman a lot. I think he's serious about her. I guess he wanted me to meet her family, which is her son."

"Cozy. So when are all of you going to get together again?"

"I don't know. I'd like to get together with Matt separately. He says he wants to see my artwork."

"Great. He noticed you're alive. That's a hopeful sign."

"*That's* a hopeful sign?"

"Sure," said Alison. "Go with it. So when are you going to see him again?"

"It hasn't been decided."

"Which means you're left hanging. You don't know if

you'll hear from him or not. Do you have a gut feeling about this?"

"No. I'm just puzzled."

"Maybe your father has some answers. Wait a week and then see if he's gotten any feedback about tonight. Meanwhile, I'm going to get off the phone and go to sleep."

"I thought your family never slept."

"That's just folklore. Good night."

"Good night, Alison."

I hoped I would dream about Matt that night and that I would remember the dream the next morning. But I woke up blank.

My father had already left for work. Betty was in the kitchen cleaning up. Betty is a religious person and she prays every day for my mother to return. She prays over the kitchen sink. Some of my mother's friends used to call Betty a gem because she's so great at housework. But I call her a gem because she's a nice lady.

"Good morning," she said. "Looks like they liked your food."

"Yeah, I was a big success. Are there any English muffins?"

"Cleaned out," said Betty. "Timmy ate the last one."

Timmy is Betty's six-year-old son. Sometimes she brings him to work. He was in the living room, watching TV. He's cute. For one of my summer projects I was planning to draw his portrait and give it to Betty as a surprise. I can do portraits without the subject posing.

I made some toast. "We're out of a lot of stuff," Betty said as she handed me some peach jam. "How'd you like to go to the supermarket after breakfast?"

"I thought you'd never ask."

Betty grinned and handed me a list of things to buy. "Start at the top," she said. "You'll be in the left aisle of the store and you'll be working your way to the right." Betty's lists were always left to right.

I shopped quickly at the supermarket. When I was at the checkout counter, I felt a tap on my shoulder. I turned around. A woman was standing behind me. I didn't recognize her.

"Hello there," she said. "Remember me? I'm Mrs. Spiegel."

It was the spray-can lady.

"How are you today?" she asked.

I hoped that wasn't the beginning of a bunch of questions.

"Fine, thanks."

"How are you going to get all of those groceries home?"

"Strong arms. I always buy too much. But I manage. Don't worry."

"I'll give you a lift. I have a car."

"No, that's okay."

"I insist."

In the car she said, "I live just a few blocks from you. In the apartment section of town. It's not like having a house."

"It's probably very nice. I mean, apartments can be nice."

"Want to see it?"

"Uh . . ."

She drove to her apartment house. In a way, I didn't mind. I didn't have anything else to do except take my groceries home. And I was getting an education. Mrs. Spiegel has a real gift. She gets you to do things you really don't want to do, but she makes you think you should do them anyway. Politicians get elected by using that kind of talent. Advertisers use it to make lots and lots of money. But Mrs. Spiegel ended up with an ordinary job going door to door.

I helped her carry her groceries into her apartment. We left my groceries in the trunk of her car. There wasn't anything that would spoil. Mrs. Spiegel's apartment was kind of plain and simple except for all the stuff on the walls. There were certificates with gold seals and silver seals, and there were plaques of various sizes. Everything had her name on it. Mrs. Opal O'Malley Spiegel. One certificate said she was Merchandiser of the Month. One said that she sold 10,000 dollars worth of products. One referred to her as a Market Research Specialist. Mrs. Spiegel must have been in plenty of businesses.

She was busy unloading her groceries. "We'll have lunch," she said.

"I just had breakfast before I went to the supermarket."

"It wasn't substantial, I'm sure. Lunch will take a while

to prepare and you'll work up an appetite. I hope you like roast chicken. I've had this bird defrosting since early this morning. It's a tender bird, young."

"Sounds fine. Can I help?"

Mrs. Spiegel rubbed the chicken with margarine. Then she gave me some carrots to peel and chop at the kitchen table. I kind of liked being with her, but I hardly knew her. It was a strange little domestic scene. The pots, the pans, the carrot scrapings, the plump little chicken lying on its margarined back, dead on the Formica counter of Mrs. Spiegel's kitchen. Somebody would think we were mother and daughter and we did this all the time.

Mrs. Spiegel put the chicken in the oven. "It will take about three quarters of an hour. Do you want to call home and tell them you're here?"

"Yeah. Betty—she's our maid—will think I got kidnapped at the supermarket."

I wasn't sure I hadn't been kidnapped.

"Give her my telephone number," said Mrs. Spiegel.

"Why? I'm not a little kid. She doesn't have to know where to reach me."

"You're a teenager, aren't you? Teenagers always want to get reached by the right person." Mrs. Spiegel winked. I think winks are old-fashioned, but I winked back and said, "Right."

After my phone call I sat down on the living-room couch while Mrs. Spiegel did things in the kitchen. Then I got up and walked around the room. A large bookcase covered most of one wall. I thumbed through some books. Then I noticed what looked like a scrapbook. I pulled it out. There was a title printed by hand on the cover: THOUGHTS BY OPAL. It looked like a personal book.

I called to Mrs. Spiegel. "Is it okay to open up 'Thoughts by Opal'?"

"Be my guest," said Mrs. Spiegel.

The first page said THOUGHTS BY OPAL. And below it, BY OPAL O'MALLEY SPIEGEL.

The second page had a title in big letters: FRAGMENTS. Then:

> *I am destined to ring doorbells forever. It is a curious and crazy kind of doom, like being adrift just beyond the world's sensibilities. Not wanted, not missed, not existing.*
>
> *I do something of consequence. I invade lives.*
>
> *Rich people have a manicured lawn of a life.*
>
> *I am efficient, assertive, authoritative, meek, humble, compliant. I am whatever the job calls for.*

I couldn't believe Mrs. Spiegel had written this stuff! It was so sad, poetic, and cynical. It sounded like it was written by a gaunt bearded man with wild eyes.

Mrs. Spiegel came into the room. "I used to write poetry for my high school magazine," she said. "But I learned early that poets have one gigantic problem. They don't eat. Years later, when I had to go to work after my husband died, and my artist romance broke up, I decided to ring doorbells for a living. Better than being trapped nine-to-five at a desk. I sold various products until I got into market research. The fragments you're reading show the depressing side of my work. But I like the challenge of what I do. I get results. So, is your father having any luck in getting a job?"

I made my confessions over Mrs. Spiegel's delicious roast chicken. About my father being a successful lawyer, and my mother not being a travel agent. She didn't seem angry that I had lied to her. "We didn't have a relationship yesterday," she said. "Now we have a relationship. I would be offended if you lied to me now."

By the end of the meal I was calling Mrs. Spiegel Opal. And I was telling her about Matt. Like I might have told my own mother if I had a mother like Opal.

"Give him two weeks," she said. "If nothing happens, you act."

"But how? I'm not sure if he even wants to see me again."

Opal didn't answer. She got up, went into the living room, pulled a book from her bookcase, and brought it back to the table. The book had a long title. Something about motivating people.

She opened to a chapter called "Reluctant Customers."

Chapter 5

Matt didn't call. He hadn't said he would. I only fantasized that he would. I had listened politely to Opal's recital of the entire chapter on reluctant customers, but I didn't use any of her hints. I didn't do anything.

But something happened. My father hired Matt to work in his office for the summer. It was one of those jobs that pay practically nothing but are in demand by students who are anxious to gain experience in their future field of work. My father told me about this a week after the dinner, the very time Alison had told me was right for trying to extract information about Matt from my father. But he told me on his own.

We were out to dinner. We try to go out once a week to eat. It has become a nice little tradition with us, a father-daughter weekly dinner at a restaurant. We take turns picking the restaurant. It was my father's turn.

The restaurant was dark, hushed, and decorated in overdone understatement. I took one look at it and winced. It had a kind of hypocritical grace. It reeked of the kind of good breeding and gentility that only money could buy. It was not the sort of place that would rally around Deborah Kerr after her mansion rotted, her crops failed, and her servants fled. Instead, it would cancel her credit until her husband, Gregory Peck, came through with proof of his newly struck oil well in El Paso.

"Fine management here," my father said. I guess he had a point. None of the diners were raucous, no one had audibly belched. My father leaned back in his silver-flecked, overdone, understated chair. "This is nice." He rubbed his eyes.

"Are you tired?"

"Very. I'm carrying my usual workload and at the same time I'm trying to break in someone new at the office. It's a strain."

"The firm took on a new lawyer?"

"Not exactly. A kind of intern, you might say. You know him. Matt Green. I arranged it. He thinks he wants to be a lawyer, so this will be good experience for him."

I felt sly. I had been getting ready to ask my father about Matt, and here was information handed to me. Now I could talk about Matt without being conspicuous.

"Will he be working for you full-time?"

"Full-time."

"Did he mention to you that he's interested in art?"

Rats! I was being conspicuous anyway.

"*Art?*"

"Remember that he wanted to see my artwork?"

My father shrugged his shoulders. I had reached a dead end.

The waiter came to take our orders. After he left I said, "How's Gossamer?"

"Splendid, I'd say. I hope you like her, Jody."

"I hardly know her. Are you serious about her?"

"She's a friend. That's about it at this stage. I'm a cautious person."

"I believe in caution. Absolutely. Uh, did they—that is, Gossamer and Matt—enjoy their dinner at our house?"

"Gossamer said you're a fine cook."

"And Matt? What did he say?"

My father looked at me. He was catching on. He was qualified in two ways to catch on. As a father and as a lawyer. My questions were transparent.

"Gossamer said they both had a pleasant evening. That's all I know about it."

I hoped Alison had some new ideas.

She did. The next day she told me to forget Matt. We were sitting in a shoe store in the mall. "I have a consolation prize for you," she said.

"Consolation prize?"

"Yep."

"Are you going to buy me a pair of sandals?"

"Better. I'm going to introduce you to R. E. Cross. He's a friend of Pete's from summer camp. He's going to visit Pete next weekend."

Pete Summers is Alison's boyfriend. They grew up on the same street.

"What's he like? Does everybody kid him that *R* stands for 'right'?"

"I don't know anything about him except that he's Pete's age and they were pals at camp. Pete hasn't seen him for several years. But they've been corresponding. Pete says he writes great letters and he was also good at catching frogs. Want to meet him?"

"With a buildup like that, no, thanks."

"He might get your mind off Matt."

"My mind's already off Matt. I'm going to lose myself in my work. I've lined up a bunch of art projects. You know Betty's little boy, Timmy? I'm doing a portrait of him. That is, I'm going to start today. That's my first project."

"I have to introduce this R.E. to somebody. He'll only be here for that weekend. Pete's already promised him a terrific Saturday night. You'd be with Pete and me too. You wouldn't have to be alone with this guy. Do me a favor. What's one night out of your whole life?"

"I'll think about it. All right, I thought about it. Yes."

"Thanks. Do these sneakers make my feet look enormous?"

When I got home, I spent three hours on Timmy's picture. After dinner I gave up. There was something wrong with the eyes. The next day when I woke up I would know what it was. When you stare at something too long, you lose perspective. It's the same as thinking about something too much. Then again, maybe I had thought too little about doing Alison that favor. I had answered too fast. I would have preferred to spend next Saturday night by myself. This was getting to be the summer of the strangers. Gossamer and Matt Green, Opal Spiegel, and now R. E. Cross.

Matt Green? Why was I thinking about him? What good would it do me? I wondered what he was doing right then. It was evening. He was probably home with his mother. Or maybe he was out on a date. I could find out. The telephone was an instrument of magic. All I had to do was dial Matt's number and I could learn if he was home or out. Then what? What if he was home? What could I say to him? I could pretend to be in Opal's business. Hello, I'm taking a survey. Do you find me aesthetically pleasing? I'm looking for an in-depth answer.

If only it were that easy! Maybe I could just call him and chat. How are you? It was nice having you for dinner. How do you like working in my father's office? Tonight he could be bored and really anxious for a friendly conversation.

My father knew Matt's telephone number, but I couldn't ask him for it. I picked up the Manhattan telephone directory and looked under Green. Green was easy to find, there were so many of them. My eyes swept down the list of Greens. I saw Green Gossamer. Now I was happy that she had that odd name. I also looked to see if a Matt Green were listed. He could have his own phone number. I didn't find it. In a vague kind of way this made me feel that he belonged to his mother.

I picked up the receiver and dialed Gossamer's number. I pretended that it was like dialing Alison's number, something I do all the time. Nothing unusual. It rang for a long time. Maybe, on the other end, Matt was in the shower or eating a late dinner. The more it rang, the more intrusive I felt.

Finally a man answered. It was Matt! I could see him with a towel wrapped around him or with a mouthful of food. But worst of all I could see myself making an absolutely silly telephone call. I should have thought of a real reason to call him. What was a good reason? Quick—think! Why wasn't I born a fast thinker? I hung up.

With the receiver back in place, I imagined I had irritated Matt. He had answered after many rings, possibly being pulled away from something he was doing. And then, click! Now I had a good reason to call him back. To apologize. Oh, sure. First he would learn that I had hung up on him. Then I would be left with making up a reason for having called him in the first place *and* hanging up. I was shaking. No way was I going to call him again.

I felt like making a safe, easy call. A call that would push the one I had just made into the background. I decided to call Opal. I had promised to call her. But really, what did we have in common? A shared chicken dinner. That was about it. If this were winter and I had school, I certainly wouldn't have time for her. She was a summer kind of experience.

She answered on the first ring. I could hear voices in

the background. She had company. I was glad. Somebody had rung *her* bell. It seemed only fair.

"Opal," I said. "I can hear that you've got company. I'll call back another time."

"Wait. How's the reluctant customer?"

"He hasn't called. He's got a job working in my father's office for the summer."

"Providential. Visit your father's office. My bell's ringing. Good-bye."

She was unsinkable. An advice-o-matic machine, patent pending. She was like a mother instinctively knowing her child. But I was my father's child. My father proudly specialized in advice that was rooted in logic. And if it were lacking in logic, at the very least it would have dignity. It wouldn't be dignified for me to visit his office just because Matt was there. But from time to time I did go to my father's office, when I shopped in the city, or when we ate together in the city, or sometimes just because I felt like it.

I felt like it.

Chapter 6

I always feel like a bug when I go into New York City. I *am* a bug when I go into New York City. I'm one of millions of creatures. Sometimes I feel like the littlest bug of them all. When I was seven I wrote a story with that title in which the bug triumphs over everybody simply by being kind.

It was easy for the bug. But being kind hadn't worked for me. I had been kind to Matt. I had served him dinner, I had talked to him, I had yearned for him. Forget the last part. Forget kind. I wasn't being kind now. I was being desperate. And I wasn't going to triumph.

On the train going into the city I tried not to think about Matt Green. I sized up the other passengers and imagined what they were going to do in the city. They were going to work. To eat. To attend lectures. To shop. To study. To fight. To see a show. To give testimonial dinners. To gossip. To visit museums. To discuss business. To take pictures. To hold a caucus. To visit. To pray. To see Matt Green. To see Matt Green? That's me. Don't think about that one.

Maybe I could talk to somebody and pass the time that way. Fat chance. I had a seat on the aisle next to a woman whose closed eyelids flickered slightly when I sat down. This was a signal to me that she was not to be counted among the dead, but I was not supposed to make any of the overtures that you usually make to the living. In other words, don't talk to her.

On the other side of the woman was a man who seemed to be assembling himself for the day, straightening his tie, smoothing his pocket flaps, cleaning his glasses. He was careful not to accidentally touch the woman and, O crime of crimes, spark a conversation. The passengers in the two rows in front of me were also sitting three abreast, silently. They were like products in a six-pack, related by having a common enclosure, but otherwise self-contained. I guess I sat down in the "No Talking" section of the train, except there isn't any.

I didn't know what I was going to do after I got to my father's office. At breakfast I had told him that I might "drop by" his office today. He was reading the newspaper, and all he said was "Fine." So here I was, on my way. I checked the contents of my pocketbook. It gave me something to do. I always take too much when I go into the city. Sunglasses, plastic rainhat, train schedule, scrap paper, pens, money, including plenty of change for buses, telephone booths, easily satisfied muggers, and sidewalk solicitors whose causes seemed worthy.

The train finally pulled into Grand Central Station. My father's office is a short walk from there. He's a partner in the law firm titled Winkleman, Hackett, Lipsert, Ives, Kline & Bradford. At last count there were twenty-three lawyers in the firm.

In the reception area there's walnut paneling, thick carpeting, and original paintings. You're supposed to be hit with a feeling of tradition, solvency, serenity, and power. No matter what your legal problem is, no matter how deep its aggravation, how dirty its details, or how many sleepless nights it has caused you, the higher powers enthroned here will relieve you of the grubby details and elevate your troubles to the refined oratory of learned gentlemen. It kind of turns me off, especially since they will also relieve you of plenty of your money. Justice paid for by unjust fees.

Sometimes I make cracks to my father about Winkleman, Hackett, Lipsert, Ives, Kline & Bradford. He reminds me that over 10 percent of their work consists of charity cases. He also tells me I'm too young to understand the marketplace value of services. Then he says that by the time I'm twenty, we won't be having this kind of conversation anymore. Maybe he's right.

Mrs. Baxter, the receptionist, smiled when she saw me. She has been with the firm for about twenty years, and she's very protective of her turf and her employers. She screens visitors so thoroughly that she can make them feel like trespassers even when they have an appointment.

"Hello, Jody. On vacation? Your father's in conference, but he should be finished soon."

"In conference" could mean my father was in the bathroom. "In conference" can mean absolutely anything, but it sounds professional to clients. Mrs. Baxter has a way of nodding you to a seat. She nodded me. But my father allows me to wander into the area where the offices are, as long as I don't bother anyone. There are a slew of offices beyond the reception area, plus several conference rooms and a law library. The library was the most logical place for Matt to be. Lawyers are always sending interns off to research old court cases so they won't have to do it themselves.

The library was at the end of a long aisle. A few lawyers hustled by me. Some of them recognized me and nodded. Some of them recognized me and didn't nod.

"Well, hi!"

Someone was talking to me. Someone had stopped to talk to me. It was one of the guys in a rush. It was Matt!

"Oh, hi, Matt."

"Visiting your father?"

"Yes."

"I'm working here for the summer."

"Dad told me."

"Well, it's good to see you again. If you'll excuse me, I have to do some background work on a case."

"Sure."

He walked on. It all happened so fast that it seemed as if it hadn't happened at all. It could go down in the record books: shortest conversation ever to take place between two people. I'd never had such a deflating experience. If he cared even a little about me, he would have talked for at least a minute. That was the end of that! Opal Spiegel's advice-o-matic machine should be junked.

My father really was in conference. I peeked into his office and saw him talking with a man and a woman. I went back to the reception area to wait for him. Maybe we could have lunch together. Maybe I could salvage the day, if not my pride.

I waited for about half an hour. I watched people come and go. I watched Mrs. Baxter, busy and important at her command post. I read some business magazines.

"Hello, stranger." It was Matt. I didn't want another friendly greeting from him. Once again he had noticed I was alive, but it was not, as Alison had described, a hopeful sign. It meant nothing.

"I'm going out for a bite. Want to come?"

An invitation. *That* I wanted. Still, it was all very accidental. I happened to be sitting in his path as he was walking out. I hesitated.

Mrs. Baxter was watching us. She would wonder why I came to see my father but left with Matt. After doing the same job for twenty years, she deserved a minimystery to confuse her working day. I left with Matt.

We went to a luncheonette not far from the office. We ordered sandwiches and sodas. I sent out a mental order to rescue Opal Spiegel's advice-o-matic machine from the trash heap.

I waited for him to speak first.

"Been busy with your artwork?"

He had remembered. And right away.

"I've started a portrait of our maid's son. It's going to be a surprise for both of them."

"Isn't he posing?"

"No, I'm doing it from memory."

"You mean you could look at me across this table and then go home and draw me from memory?"

"Yeah."

Here was his chance to ask again to see my pictures. Instead, he suddenly changed the subject. He started to laugh.

"What's so funny?"

"I shouldn't tell you this, but this morning a woman came in carrying a ripped trick-or-treat shopping bag overflowing with papers. What's more, she was wearing a T-shirt and army boots. Well, she demands to see Mr. Winkleman. He agrees to see her. They're quite a pair. He's very correct, you know. Wouldn't remove his tie or jacket if he were stuck in the Sahara. She tells him she's upset about the way the firm is handling her late husband's estate. It seems that she spends her spare time reading law books about estate situations. She begins citing precedents to Mr. Winkleman. Well, the precedents are off the mark just enough to have no bearing on her situation, but close enough to cause Mr. Winkleman to excuse himself. I think he went to the law library or the john. I'm just standing there, but she ignores me with a vengeance, sizing me up as a junior, and she knows the

blood flows reddest at the top. She gets impatient waiting for Mr. Winkleman to return, she scribbles something on a piece of paper, hands it to me, and marches
out."

Matt was laughing again, so I laughed.

"That was really a funny story," I said.

"I'm not finished."

"Oh. Well, I know you're not finished. But it's funny *so
far*. Go on."

He was looking at me as if he didn't believe me. He
figured he had a good story and the wrong audience. I
wish people would signal when they're finished telling a
funny story.

"Go on," I urged him again.

"Okay. Here's what she wrote on the paper. 'Dear Mr.
Winkleman. I am appalled at the manner in which your
firm is handling my husband's estate. When you return
from wherever you are, ponder these words:

> " 'I think that there will never be
> An impetus as strong for me
> To be the first of man or beast
> Never to become deceased.' "

Should I laugh? I thought it was funny. But what if
there were just a little more? What if I laughed as if he
were finished and he wasn't? Once is bad enough, but
twice and he would be insulted. I sat there waiting for
him to laugh. He did. I did.

He had more stories. I could see that this was going to

be a friendly little chirpy-happy lunch and he was not going to ask to see me again. Maybe he thought I was too young for him. Maybe it was inconvenient for him to date somebody who lived in the suburbs. Maybe he had a girlfriend. Or the newest possibility, maybe he thought I had no sense of humor.

I felt the same way about him that I did when I met him. He looked a little different, older, I think. But I always expect a person to look different the second time. It's the artist in me. One time you get one angle, the next time you get another angle. Also, lighting and clothing and mood change a person's appearance.

"Want to see my artwork?"

I didn't say that. I couldn't have said that. I know where the words came from. Opal Spiegel. I was possessed by her. Still, that wasn't exactly what she would have said. She would have said, "I'll expect you at my house in five minutes to see my artwork." If that didn't get results, she would proceed with, "You can't imagine what I, as an artist, go through. The world, cold and unappreciative, will revere me when I'm dead. What good will that do me? I can't eat postmortem groceries. Appreciate me now. It will make up for my unheated attic home, the rats, my hacking cough . . ."

"Yes, of course, I want to see your artwork. But I can't."

"You *can't?* There's a law?"

"Let me explain, Jody. Your father and my mother are very, very serious about each other."

"That isn't what he told me. And, anyway, what does that have to do with your seeing my pictures?"

"Simple. I don't want to encourage my mother to marry your father."

"He's not divorced," I said.

"But he's getting there. You know that."

"Okay. So?"

"Before Mom met your father, she was so close to remarrying my dad that they were practically at the altar again. And they *should* remarry. They were meant to be together. Remember how much Mom talked about Dad at your house? Now, if I take you out, which I'd like to do . . ."

Which he'd like to do!

"I almost asked you the other night. But my mother would have thought, well, isn't this just perfect—all of us getting along so well. Gerald, me, our kids hitting it off. Jody, I *know* my mother. She just needs a *sign,* a signal, to commit to your father. Don't get me wrong. I like your father, and I appreciate the opportunity he's giving me this summer. But I want my folks back together again."

"I don't buy that. I mean, your life is your own."

Opal Spiegel, you'd be proud of me.

I kept going. "Some day my pictures will hang in a gallery and you'll have to pay to see them, or at least pay to own one. So you don't have to see them now or take me out or anything. Forget it. But what if your mother gives equal weight to her horoscope sign or the right word from her hairdresser or—or her clothing designer?

What makes you think her future is hanging on what *you* do?"

Matt was grinning. "Have you undergone a personality change? You were so quiet at dinner. Well, not when you had that little flare-up with your father. But other than that, you hardly said a word."

"Maybe I picked up a role model."

"How's that?"

"Oh, nothing. Actually, I hope I haven't picked up a role model. I just want to be myself."

"Would yourself like to go out with me next Saturday night? I'll get tickets to something."

"You don't have to ask me out. I didn't mean to shoot my mouth off. Look, I went too far."

"Can I pick you up at seven?"

"You sound as if you mean it."

"Sure, I mean it."

"Well, okay, seven will be great."

I couldn't begin to tell Matt how great it would be. I was going to see him again!

We walked back to the office. I went out to lunch again. With my father. Mrs. Baxter heard me thank Matt for lunch about ten minutes before I swept past her reception desk with my father as he asked, "Where would you like to go for lunch?" I looked back to see if she was mouthing the word *"lunch?"*

I enjoyed having lunch with my father even though I couldn't eat much. He suggested that I stay in town and we could go to a Rocky movie that night. A fight picture.

Something was trying to connect with something else in my brain. It had to do with a fight. Suddenly "right cross," as in R. E. Cross, came into focus. I had a date with R. E. Cross for next Saturday night. I had a date with Matt Green for next Saturday night.

I certainly wasn't going to break the date with Matt. Alison would understand about my backing out. Wouldn't she? She had really pressured me into saying yes in the first place.

I never make wise decisions in shoe stores.

Chapter 7

Alison understood. But not totally, fully, or without reservations. There was a hitch.

"Sure, I understand," she said when I told her the next day. "You forgot you had a date with R.E. when you accepted Matt. You probably forgot what your name was when you accepted Matt. It's exciting and I'm really happy for you. But . . . Pete already told R.E. that he got a fantastic date for him. He praised you to the skies. So now all you need is a fantastic replacement."

"But . . ."

"Don't worry, a less than fantastic replacement will do. But, Jody, I do need somebody. This guy's coming to town expecting a great date and a great time next Saturday night. He's already been promised that."

"Does Pete know anybody?"

"Pete? I'm not even going to tell him you backed out until I can present him with a new girl. Any ideas, Jody?"

"Lots. How about Heather Rollins? She's cute, she's fun, she's bright, and she's . . . away for the summer. I just remembered."

"Yeah, too bad. I would have picked her first too. How about one of the Lindas? I heard that Linda Zalt is going steady. But Linda Johnson . . . she might be fine. Jody, you should call Linda Johnson."

"Me?"

"Who else? You're looking for a replacement for *you.*"

"You're making this tough for me. You know Linda better than I do. Never mind. I'll do it. And if she turns me down, I'll try Victoria. Okay?"

"Victoria? Sure. We've got plenty of candidates. But Linda will probably say yes right away."

Linda said no. Right after she asked for a description of R. E. Cross and unfortunately all I could remember was something about frogs. But I assured her he had probably given up frogs a long time ago. Linda is someone who deliberates over every little decision. But this time she said no right away.

I called Victoria. She was on a camping trip in Maine.

I called Alison back. "Listen, we'll think of someone by tomorrow," she said. "Or the next day. My head's at work on it and will continue to be at work on it."

"I'd like to settle this by tomorrow," I said. "It's like a hangnail. I want to get rid of it."

I thought about girls most of the day and evening. I made up a list of girls I knew and hardly knew and didn't know at all. Then I disqualified most of them. One was going steady, one was a creep, one had just moved away. And then there was Tanya. Tanya Lipsert. Tanya is the daughter of one of my father's law partners. That fact alone should have made us friends. We're about the same age too. But there was something at work behind her green eyes and sweet smile that bothered me. There was something a little *off* about Tanya, as if she were operating from an angle, a vantage point, a pose. But now I was thinking that she had two wonderful assets: She wasn't away for the summer, and she didn't have a steady boyfriend. I decided to phone her first thing the next morning.

The next morning I wondered if six A.M. was too early to call Tanya Lipsert. Maybe. No point in getting her mad. If I waited until nine and called her then, by nine fifteen my little problem would probably be solved. I went back to sleep.

Betty woke me at ten when she tiptoed to my door to see if I was awake. "A postcard from your mother," she said. "Want me to read it to you?"

My mother's postcards weren't private affairs. My father and Betty and I were so used to them that it was taken for granted that Betty could read them even though they were addressed only to "Gerald and Jody dears."

"This one's from Denmark," said Betty. Then she read, " 'Copenhagen is dear and delightful, especially the third time around. Kiss yourselves for me. Love always, Sue.' "

Betty sighed. "Will she never come home? I'm just looking for that card that says 'coming home.' I haven't given up hope. Or my prayers. Prayers are powerful. They'll save her. They'll bring her back."

I don't like to discourage sincere people with deep convictions, so I just nodded. Nothing would bring my mother back unless she ran out of money. But she had a huge inheritance from *her* mother. I wondered what my mother looked like now, if she'd changed much in the two years she'd been gone. I wanted her to come home, but I had given up hope. Still, I wasn't going to live out my life without seeing her again. I had a kind of general plan that, when I got a little older, I'd take a trip and try to catch up with her someplace. The plan was really general, because I never knew where she was until we received mail from her, and by then she might have gone elsewhere. However, she was being sent money, so somebody knew her itinerary. Maybe it was just a clerk in a bank. I don't know how these things work. Somehow I think my father knew, but he wasn't saying. There was this divorce business and his being a lawyer, and it added up that he knew. Sometimes I wondered if he'd take my mother back. It was hard to tell. After the first year, he had stopped talking about her coming back. His sense of self had taken over. And now Gossamer had taken over.

The postcard made me forget that it was ten o'clock, three quarters of an hour past the time when my problem was supposed to have been solved. Then I remembered and felt panicky. What if Tanya Lipsert had gone out for the entire day? Life is strange. The morning before, I hadn't cared what Tanya Lipsert was doing. I wouldn't have cared if she had moved out of the country. I wouldn't have given her one thought. It's terrifying how your life can take these turns. Tomorrow I might be frantically hoping for something that seems so insignificant today. I might hope that a certain flower will grow in my yard or that the mail will arrive before ten o'clock. Why would I care about these things? I don't know. But they aren't any more remote than having Tanya Lipsert suddenly become a pivotal point in my life. This might be a mildly interesting phenomenon to bring up in my philosophy class this fall, if I can do it without mentioning Tanya Lipsert's name.

Betty was still standing there. "Ready for breakfast?" she asked.

"In a while. I have to make a phone call first."

Betty left. She was rereading the postcard and shaking her head as she walked away.

I picked up the telephone receiver. Good move. I didn't know what number to dial. Tanya Lipsert's telephone number was not exactly engraved in my memory. I looked it up. Then I was ready.

I dialed the number. She answered! She was home. I was thinking that it was very nice of her to be home. I was not thinking clearly. You should not give a person credit just for being in her own house.

"Hi, Tanya. This is Jody."

I didn't include my last name. That made it seem friendlier, like it was more natural for me to be calling her.

"Jody? Oh, yes, Jody."

"So, how's your summer going?"

"Great."

Did that mean she had a boyfriend?

"Uh, I'm calling you because, well, maybe I can make your summer even greater. How would you like to go out on a blind date?"

"When?"

"Next Saturday night."

"Oh."

She didn't say she was busy. She just seemed to be thinking about it. Finally she said, "What's he like?"

How stupid could I be! After flunking out with Linda Johnson because I couldn't give R.E. a good buildup, I should have quizzed Alison about him, or even called Pete. If you're trying to sell something, you should at least have some sales materials.

I remembered what Alison had said about R.E. being good at writing letters and catching frogs. "Well, versatile would be an accurate way to describe this guy. He's a brilliant writer and he's also an outdoor person. Very interested in nature and nature's creatures. Versatile is what R. E. Cross is all about."

"R.E.? Doesn't he have a regular first name?"

"I'm sure he does. But he goes by this because, well, you know how writers are. Sometimes they use initials instead of their first name. He's really just terrific."

I had gone too far. Overkill is never a good idea.

"You're anxious for me to go out with him, aren't you?"

Tanya sensed something. I think it was my desperation. She went on. "Make me want to go out with him."

There it was. The angle. The something about Tanya that kept me from liking her. She wanted me to beg her to go out on this date. If I said please or something like that, she'd be satisfied. She'd say yes.

"You'd be going out with Alison and Pete too," I said. "And you know they're lots of fun."

"Not enough."

Not enough fun or not enough incentive? I didn't know what she meant, but I wasn't going any further. I wasn't going to plead.

"It's up to you," I said, knowing the words would cost me.

"I guess I'll have to answer in the negative, Jody. Your offer just doesn't grab me. But I'm sure you'll find some other lucky girl."

"I'm sure I will. Well, continue to have a great summer." I hung up. Is it hanging up in somebody's face if you don't wait for them to say good-bye? I hoped so. If I had only given Tanya what she wanted, my problem would have been solved. But I couldn't.

I looked at my list of girls. I didn't have much faith in it. But I had to keep trying.

I called three more girls. One didn't answer, one had a virus, and one was Amy Vincetti. Amy was pleasant, friendly, and she didn't ask me what R.E. was like. She was a joy to talk to after my experience with Tanya. I told her it would be a double date with Alison and Pete. Everything seemed fine to her. She was enthusiastic. How come I had never noticed until this moment that her voice was angelic, her diction perfect, and that she was an altogether fabulous person? There were no words to describe how wonderful she was. She said she'd love to go, but . . .

But? Please, no!

She said she'd have to call me back, because she had promised to baby-sit next Saturday night if the neighbors needed her. They were supposed to let her know in a day or so.

"A day or so? Could that even be today?"

"Could be. I'll let you know the minute I know. It was sweet of you to think of me, and it would be fun to go out with Alison and Pete and this R.E."

Amy was grateful. Why hadn't I called her before I called Tanya? Because she'd had a crush on Pete Summers for years. Alison knew that. There was no danger that Amy could take Pete away from Alison, but still, Alison was wary of Amy. Alison would not be crazy about double-dating with her.

I called Alison. By this time I was hungry. Maybe I'd skip breakfast and just eat lunch.

"Alison, I think I've got somebody to go out with R.E. You're not going to be overjoyed, but it was the best I could do. It's Amy Vincetti."

"Amy? You called Amy? She'll be thrilled to spend an evening in Pete's company."

"Honestly, I tried others. And it's not definite with Amy. She might have to baby-sit. She'll let me know in a day or so."

Alison laughed. "You just set off a chain reaction whether you know it or not. Amy is now phoning other girls to see if she can get a replacement for *herself* for her baby-sitting job. When you said yes to Matt Green you really started something."

"I hope it ends soon. I guess I'll just wait for Amy to call me."

"Have faith. She'll see to it that she's available."

"Are you angry at me for getting her?"

"No. It's okay. Pete thinks she's pesty. Maybe R.E. will like her."

As I ate lunch I had a comforting vision of Amy Vincetti frantically phoning girls all over town to line them up for her baby-sitting job in case it came through. Her crush on Pete Summers, which had meant nothing to me, now was important in my life. Another remote thing had become pivotal. These shifts were getting scary.

I began to think about what I would wear when I went out with Matt. Maybe I'd get my hair cut. It was getting draggy on my shoulders. Perhaps I'd buy a new pair of shoes. It was nice to think about all the preparations. I kept dreaming up more and more things to do to get ready.

I dialed Opal's number. She deserved to be told the good news. She was responsible for my going to New York City and seeing Matt. There wasn't any answer. She was probably out ringing doorbells.

I went shopping for a new dress. I went by myself. I like to make up my own mind about my own clothes. I found a bright yellow dress. "This dress smiles," the salesperson said.

"A smiling dress, why not?" I said, and I bought it.

I decided against new shoes. I went back to the shoe store where I had told Alison I would go out with R.E. But I couldn't find any shoes I liked better than what I already owned. A fat lady was sitting in the seat where I had been sitting when I told Alison I'd go out with R.E. She'd probably buy shoes that were too small for her. She was sitting in the seat of wrong decisions.

Betty was still at work when I got home. She and Timmy were in the kitchen. Timmy was drinking soda. I could see his big eyes over his glass. Now I knew what was wrong with the eyes in my portrait. I'd fix them.

"Any calls?" I asked.

"No," said Betty.

"Have you been inside all the time? I'm expecting an important call."

"I haven't stepped out," said Betty. "Nobody called. Buy something new?"

I opened the box I was carrying and held up the yellow dress. "Pretty dress," said Timmy. Kids like bright colors.

"You'll look beautiful in it," said Betty. Betty was so loyal and supportive, she'd say I looked beautiful in a shopping bag.

I went to my room. Should I call Amy Vincetti? No, she'd call me. Have faith.

A day went by. Two days went by. Next Saturday night had become *this* Saturday night. It was Tuesday. Only about four days left until Saturday night. I called Amy.

"What's new?" I asked casually.

"I still don't know about Saturday night," she said. "I'm still waiting to see if they need me for baby-sitting. That's why I haven't called you."

Amy didn't sound like a person who had been frantically calling all over town for a substitute baby-sitter.

I took the plunge. "Maybe you could get someone to take your place?"

"Oh, no. I couldn't do that. I've been taking care of this little kid for months. She's only two years old. I know her. She knows me. It's an almost steady job, and I wouldn't back out unless I was sick or something."

"You're a dependable person, Amy." I hoped I was hiding how I really felt. Frustrated, absolutely frustrated.

"Thanks. And you can depend on me to call you just as soon as I know anything."

"Right. Good-bye."

I couldn't be mad at Amy. She was doing everything right. Now my Saturday night depended on whether Amy's neighbors were or were not going out. Their plans were probably dependent on somebody else's plans.

Maybe it was crazy to wait for Amy any longer. I called Alison. It seemed as if I was always calling Alison these days. I told her I was getting impatient with the Amy situation. "I wasn't waiting for Amy," she said. "I made a couple of calls just in case. I figured we could tell Amy that we couldn't wait any longer."

"Wonderful! So who'd you get?"

"Nobody. I struck out. Did you know that a virus is going around?"

After I hung up I made one more call. I found out that a virus certainly was going around. I called two sick twins I hardly knew.

On Thursday Amy called to say her baby-sitting job was definite. Irrationally I felt mad at a two-year-old kid who couldn't take care of herself.

I found myself calling Opal. She would tell me what I wanted to hear: "You did your best for your friend Alison. You absolutely gave it your best shot. *Shots.* You knocked yourself out trying. Go out with Matt Green."

Opal was home. I told her everything that had happened. I told her I had a decision to make. I waited for her words, "Go out with Matt Green."

Instead she said, "I'll quote to you from a page of 'Thoughts by Opal.' It's my newest." She put down the receiver. She was back in a few seconds.

"Remember when you called me the other night and I had company? I was throwing a little cocktail party. One of my guests couldn't decide among my miniature wieners in sesame rolls, my salami cornucopias, my gherkins stuffed with nut meats, and my mushrooms stuffed with shad roe. He just stood there trying to make up his mind. I rushed to my book and wrote something in honor of the occasion. It's perfect for your problem too."

Opal raised her voice slightly. " 'There is no such thing as the right decision,' " she read. " 'There are only decisions that, having been made, move harmoniously and fortuitously in the course of time with the vagaries of chance, and thus become, in retrospect, the right decision."

Opal waited for my reaction.

"It would go nicely with a flute accompaniment," I said.

Opal O'Malley Spiegel was in her poetic mood, and I was out of luck.

Chapter 8

Alison was sympathetic but firm.

"R.E. has only one night in town," she said, "and he's expecting a date. Only one night. You can go out with Matt next week. Or the week after. He'll be around all summer. Pete will be mad at me if I disappoint his friend. Remember, you said yes to me before Matt Green ever asked you out."

Alison couldn't make me go out with R.E. She'd cool down eventually if I broke the date. We'd had fights before. None of them had lasted very long.

"I'll let you know soon," I said.

I could confide in my father. My father knew that Matt had taken me to lunch. And he was kind of interested in Matt and me because of the Gossamer connection. But I remembered that I had been in a situation once before where I had accidentally made two appointments for the same time and gone to my father for advice. He advised me that I had entered into two contracts and the earlier one took precedence over the later one. That wasn't much help to me.

I called Matt Green at work. I didn't want to call him at home. I didn't want to call him at work, either, but I had made my decision. I got through to him immediately. I spoke quickly because it was easier that way. "Matt, I'm awfully sorry but I have to break our date for this Saturday night. I know it's short notice—"

"I got tickets."

I didn't want to hear that. It made everything so much worse. But I went on. "What happened is that I had promised my friend Alison that I would go out with her boyfriend's friend who will be in town for only that one night. When you asked me out, I completely forgot about it. Anyway, when I remembered, I tried to find another girl to take my place. But no luck. Perhaps you've heard about the virus in our neighborhood?"

Matt was silent.

"I can't begin to tell you how sorry I am. Could you turn in the tickets for another night? I'm free all summer except for this one Saturday night."

"I see."

"Do you?"

"Yeah."

I waited for Matt to make another date. I was expecting too much. He didn't say anything. It was so awkward. My excuse sounded so lame to my ears. It must have sounded even worse to Matt. He didn't know about all the work I had done to try to keep the date.

I repeated how sorry I was. I couldn't keep saying I was sorry. But he wasn't asking me for another date. There wasn't any input from him. So at last I said, "Good-bye," and he said, "Good-bye," and that was that.

It wasn't anything worth crying over, but after I hung up I cried. It was all so frustrating, so unnecessary. Somewhere along the way something had gone wrong. I had said yes to Alison too soon. I had failed to say please to Tanya Lipsert. Amy Vincetti had decided she was irreplaceable. The virus had caught up with several girls but had not touched Amy's neighbors, which would have forced them to cancel her. Fate twists and turns you, and I had this premonition of Amy calling me at the last minute to say that her neighbors had canceled and she was available. Now I knew firsthand how people go insane, how raving maniacs are created from scratch.

Amy didn't call, and by the time Saturday night came around I had psyched myself up to be a good sport and a good date. I even wore my new yellow dress.

Chapter 9

R.E. Cross—R. for Reuben—had outgrown his frog stage. He was a husky, athletic-looking guy with a strong face and a ruddy complexion. I think he was pleasantly surprised when he saw me. He should have been. I had taken as much care to get ready as I would have for Matt Green. It was part of my good-sport frame of mind.

Pete had recently got his driver's license, and the four of us went out in his family's car. "You'll never guess what we're going to do tonight," Pete said as he drove along. The remark was addressed to Alison and me, because R.E. already knew what we were going to do.

"We're having a night picnic," said R.E. "Ever been on one? It's such a neat thing to do."

I had never been on a night picnic, and I was content to leave it that way. I wasn't dressed for a picnic. We were now about a mile from my house. I could ask Pete to turn around so I could go home and change into jeans and a shirt. There were picnic grounds in the area, complete with splintery benches and tables. Just my luck that I would snag my new dress on splinters.

I didn't ask Pete to turn around. And I didn't have to worry about splinters. I had to worry about dirt. We passed by the picnic grounds and went to a wooded area with no tables. "In order to enjoy a night picnic, you have to renounce civilization," R.E. announced as he and Pete unloaded stuff from the car.

I'm not one of those princess types. But I don't like to wear a new dress to a picnic. A scene flashed through my head. I was sitting next to Matt in my new dress. We were at a concert or a movie or whatever he had bought tickets to. We were not renouncing civilization. We were part of it. The seats we were sitting in had backs. Would I be fantasizing too much if I imagined they had armrests too?

The scene stopped abruptly as Pete opened a blanket and spread it on the ground. The blanket was full of holes and had dog hair all over it. "My folks use this when they take our dog out in the car. It protects the car seats," Pete explained. "It needed a washing anyway, so they let me use it tonight."

Pete and R.E. unpacked the food. Pete had supplied all of it. I wished he had asked me for a contribution. That way I would have learned we were going on a picnic. I slapped a mosquito, and the night was just beginning. Do ants come out in the night? Tiny, unidentifiable crawling and flying things do. The moon came out and it was full. A night for romance or madness.

"This is a super idea," said Alison. She was wearing jeans. She almost always wears jeans.

"Isn't it," said Pete. "White or dark chicken, Jody?"

"White."

This was my second unexpected chicken of the summer. Opal Spiegel's was better. Pete's came from several take-out containers, and it was coated with crispy stuff and grease.

"Napkins, anyone?" I asked. I was wondering if there were any.

"Just use your dress," said Pete, and he laughed.

R.E. handed me a paper napkin. Then he opened cans of soda.

I wasn't upset when chicken grease got on my dress. I was resigned to it happening before it happened. I knew that drops of soda would spill on my dress too. Picnics are messy. Usually that's half the fun. My dress looked luminous under the moon. Tomorrow, under the fluorescent light in my kitchen, I would be counting grease spots, soda spills, and grass stains while I plucked dog hairs.

R.E. asked me a few questions about my school and my interests and my hobbies. I asked him a few questions about his school and his interests and his hobbies.

Then Pete started to swap remember-when stories with R.E. Alison slid over next to me on the blanket and said, "Isn't this fun! All of us together!"

The stories went on and on. Alison was fascinated. She howled with laughter, howling being a good thing to do, I suppose, under a full moon. One story seemed to be worth a smile, but generally I don't find underwear on a flagpole hilarious.

Slowly it was dawning on me what the evening was all about. Alison was completely missing the point. We weren't all together. Pete and R.E. were together, and Alison and I were together. The evening was a continuation of the grand reunion between R.E. and Pete. Alison and I were on the sidelines. I didn't really blame Pete and R.E. They hadn't seen each other for years, and they were lost in the nostalgia of it. But here I was, ignored, greased, dog-hairy, slapping mosquitoes, starting to shiver because it was getting cold, and dreaming about the kind of evening it might have been with Matt. Maybe I could call Matt tomorrow and invite *him* out. That would prove that I really was sorry about breaking the date with him. He would never believe *how* sorry I was!

"I'm cold," I said.

"Want my sweater?" R.E. asked.

I didn't want his sweater. I wanted to go home. I slapped a mosquito.

"No, thanks, that's okay. But it's kind of damp and dark out here, and we're through eating."

I was breaking up their wonderful evening.

Alison said, "Take R.E.'s sweater. You don't want to leave now. R.E.'s only in town for this one night."

If I heard "R.E.'s only in town for this one night" one more time, I would strangle somebody. Probably Alison.

I took the sweater and wrapped it around me.

"Put it on," said Alison. She was attending to all the

details that would keep Pete and R.E.'s reunion intact. She might grow up to be another Mrs. Baxter, firm but gracious guardian and protector of busy men.

I put on the sweater. It looked stupid over my dress. I could tell without looking. Not that I was interested in my appearance.

"Isn't that much better?" said Alison.

She was more annoying than R.E. or Pete. They were oblivious to me. She was determined to take care of me like I was a sick flower in this thriving garden of joy.

Even though Alison and I are best friends, we are not truly alike. If we were, she would have been aware that I had traded an evening with a guy I was crazy about for a night of oblivion in mosquitoland.

"I'm really cold," I said fifteen minutes later.

"It is a little chilly," said Alison. She turned to R.E. and Pete. I knew she was about to apologize for slowly freezing to death.

"Guys, we're cold. I'm sorry. Aren't you cold?"

"You wanna go?" asked Pete.

"Well . . ."

We packed up everything. Alison suggested that we stop somewhere for a hot drink, but I said I was tired. Pete drove to my house. He and R.E. sang camp songs along the way. R.E. walked me to my door. He told me that he had enjoyed my company. I told him that I had enjoyed his company. I hoped he wasn't one of those guys who automatically kiss girls good night at the end of a date. I wasn't going to kiss him. I got busy unlocking my door, which wasn't locked. When he saw that I could open the door, he said, "So long," and he walked down the steps.

I walked into my house to find my father and Gossamer Green sitting stiffly side by side on the couch. They were sitting so stiffly apart that I figured they must have been cozily together when they heard Pete's car drive up.

"Early evening?" my father asked.

Chapter 10

My father and Gossamer unposed themselves and relaxed. They were staring at me. I must have been a sight. Rats! I was still wearing R.E.'s sweater.

"We were on a picnic and it got cold," I said. That explained my early evening and also why I was wearing a boy's sweater.

Gossamer was disheveled too. I had interrupted a necking session, or whatever adults call it, between my father and Gossamer. This was a crazy reverse situation. Usually the parent sizes up the teenager for signs of an erotic night. I had just come in from an evening so devoid of romance that—

Gossamer interrupted my thoughts. "It's fun being a teenager on a Saturday night, isn't it," she said.

Tonight it seemed to be more fun being a middle-ager.

"Matt loves Saturday nights. Of course, he won't be a teenager much longer. You didn't run into him, did you? He went to a play in this area."

Matt went out? With whom? I wanted to know. I didn't want to know.

"Seems he had this extra ticket," said my father, "and he was offering it around the office. Fred Lipsert said his daughter might be interested in going to a play. I didn't know Fred had matchmaker instincts."

"Matt took Tanya Lipsert to a play?"

"Last I heard," said my father. "How did we get on this subject? I want to know if *you* had a nice evening."

My father had obviously shrugged off my interest in Matt as a bit of trivia. Otherwise he would have realized the impact his information had on me. While I was slapping mosquitoes, Matt Green was watching a play with Tanya Lipsert. Maybe they were still out on their date. Maybe they were kissing at this very moment. I had never felt so jealous in my life.

"Did you know that your dress is stained?" Gossamer asked.

I looked down. My dress was actually streaked with stuff.

"Wild evening?" she asked.

Was she trying to embarrass me out of malice or just out of stupidity?

"Jody doesn't have wild evenings," my father said. He looked irritated.

"Oh, come on," said Gossamer.

"Excuse me," I said. I went up to my room.

My father was getting serious with Gossamer. I didn't care if he dated her, but I didn't want him to marry her. My life was fine just the way it was. Just my father and me. I loved my father even though I didn't love everything about him. We disagreed about too many things. I knew he was marking time until I grew up and became more like him. He anticipated about five more years of fights between us.

I wished I could break his Gossamer habit. That's what she was for my father, a habit. Just the way Alison and Pete were a habit. Pete was such a jerk. At the picnic he had been at his peak, but Alison hadn't even noticed. My father didn't seem to notice Gossamer's faults either. If I could only introduce him to someone else. Some of my friends had unattached mothers, but I couldn't bring my friends into this. Too sticky.

I went to bed, but I tossed and turned. In the midst of tossing and turning I remembered that I knew one unattached woman who wasn't attached to any of my friends either. Opal Spiegel. But the idea of her and my father together was just too ridiculous.

Usually the clear bright light of morning tells you the truth about ideas formed the night before. The next morning I expected the idea of Opal and my father to seem even more dumb by daylight. But it didn't. It was becoming almost credible.

I compared Opal Spiegel to Gossamer Green. They were about the same age. Opal looked as if she accepted the age. Gossamer looked as if she was fighting it. What did they have in common? Opal rang doorbells, and Gossamer . . . didn't ring doorbells. Forget the comparisons. Opal and Gossamer were not alike. Opal would have to wow my father in her own unique way. But face it,

Opal wasn't going to wow my father. She was a pushy, manipulative, warm person, but my father wasn't going to get past the first two qualities to find the third. He wasn't going to get past the fact that she rang doorbells for a living. The father I loved dearly was a snob.

I got up. I looked around my room. The night before was staring me in the face. My yellow dress and R.E.'s sweater were draped over a chair. Last night had really happened. Forget last night. Today would be better. After breakfast I would call Matt. And *not* hang up!

I heard noises coming from downstairs. My father was probably making breakfast. I was afraid to go down and join him. I was afraid he was going to make some kind of announcement about himself and Gossamer Green. Usually Sunday breakfast is my favorite breakfast of the week. My father and I have plenty of time together, and we sit around and eat too much.

I went downstairs. My father was boiling eggs. He was dressed in a crisp sport shirt. He looked relaxed, kind of edited, as if all his problems had been removed and only the good things remained. I hoped he'd let me eat before he told me the good news about himself and Gossamer.

"Are you and Gossamer getting married?"

How could I get a bite down if I didn't know?

My father smiled. He turned away from the eggs and sat down at the kitchen table. I sat down too. "Were you up all night thinking about this?" he asked.

"Well . . ."

"Jody, you have too much time to think. You're alone too much."

Here it comes. A mommy to keep Jody company.

"I'm not alone. I have you. And Betty's here four days a week. I spend a lot of time with Betty. And don't tell me she's hired help. She's like family. And most of the time I'm in school anyway. And there are clubs and meetings and friends. Also, I'm fifteen, and in a couple of years I might be on my own. College, art school, whatever. So if you're making any plans because of *me*, forget it."

"Did you rehearse that?"

"No!"

My father sighed. "All right, I'll tell you as much as there is to tell you. I'm not plunging into anything, any decisions. I've already told you that I'm proceeding with caution."

"Proceeding with caution doesn't sound like love to me."

"I don't want to mislead you, Jody. If things go along as they have been, I'll probably marry Gossamer Green."

Matt had been right. He had seen beyond my father's caution into the future. And the future was my father marrying Gossamer.

"When?" I asked.

My father laughed. "First of all, Jody, I'm not divorced. But recently, through intermediaries, I've been in contact with your mother. She appears to be willing to get a divorce. That's not the same as saying she has agreed. No matter, this could take a long time. So don't load yourself up with worries now. How about a change of subject. Would you like some eggs?"

After I ate, I went back to my room and stretched out on my bed. I looked at my watch. It was too early to call Matt. And I wasn't in the mood anyway. I was depressed about my father and Gossamer. But there was nothing I could do. I closed my eyes. I felt as if I wanted to sleep the summer through and wake up to the kind of new, bright, leafy fall that is supposed to resuscitate everybody's life. I felt aimless. I was out of work, unemployed. For about a week my goal in life had been to find someone to go out with R. E. Cross. It was employment of sorts. It kept me off the streets, it kept me anxious, quivering, and alive. Now I had no goal. My summer art projects were lined up in my head. But they were marooned there. I couldn't concentrate. I couldn't even make my phone call to Matt.

I got up and took Timmy's picture from my closet, where I kept it. At least I could finish that. I worked on the picture for half an hour. At last I knew I had it. I had captured Timmy, I had accomplished something. The next day I would give the picture to Betty and Timmy when they came in.

I started to sketch on a blank sheet in my sketchbook. I worked faster and faster. I couldn't believe what I was doing. A face was emerging. It was Matt's. I couldn't stop myself. I worked on the picture for four hours. Then I put it in the closet.

I fell on my bed, exhausted, and I let my mind drift. I

thought again about introducing Opal to my father. If I was going to have a stepmother, it would be better to pick her out myself. But the idea now seemed totally foolish. My father had grown too close to Gossamer. I was spending my day cleverly—drawing a picture that no one but me would ever see, and thinking about a meeting that would never take place.

I heard the doorbell ring. Who would be at our door on a Sunday? Alison, of course, eager to talk about and recapture all the rapture of last night's picnic. I went to the head of the stairs. I heard my father open the door and say, "I hope I didn't spoil your Sunday."

I heard someone answer, "Not at all. I prefer working here. If we tried to finish this at the office with all the interruptions, it could take a week."

"Exactly," said my father. "Come in."

Matt Green walked into my house.

Chapter 11

I couldn't believe it. Matt was in my house. Why hadn't my father told me he was coming? Why should he? Every once in a while people from his law firm come by, socially or for business. No big deal. But here was my chance to see Matt without calling him, without making a move. I was glad I hadn't tried to call him that morning.

I heard my father and Matt go into the den, which is actually my father's office at home. I went back to my room, brushed my hair, and tried to decide whether or not to change my clothes. They were slightly wrinkled from my lying on the bed. No, I wasn't going to do anything. Matt coming into my house was so natural that I was going to be natural too. I was just hanging around my own house, exactly where I should be, casual and calm. It's lucky no one can *see* your heart beating.

I walked downstairs, keeping in mind that these were my stairs and this was my house. I walked to the den and stood in the doorway. My father was sitting at his desk. Matt had pulled up a chair to sit beside him. They were going over some papers.

My father looked up. "Did we disturb you, Jody? Matt brought over some work."

Matt looked up. "Hi," he said. He looked so terrific in a beautiful blue shirt. Didn't he know that on Sundays you're allowed to lower your standards? I wished I had changed my clothes.

I said, "Hi." I knew I was in the way. They had work to do. I guess I had expected Matt to get up, come over, and say something. But he just sat there. I wanted to watch him work. I wanted to study him. But I couldn't invite myself in. If I were the family dog, I could have walked right in, sat down, and stayed. But I was a person, an awkward person, just standing in a doorway with nothing to do.

"See you later," I said, and I went into the kitchen. I poured some coffee and tried to figure out what to do next. I could go back up to my room. But what if Matt finished his work and left, just like that? If I stayed downstairs I might see him when he was through with his work. Maybe he and my father would come into the kitchen and eat something. The kitchen was definitely the place for me to be. But I had nothing to do in the kitchen. I wasn't hungry. My father and I were going out for dinner, so I didn't have a dinner to make. I could clean things up a bit, but that was a ten-minute job at most. Betty kept our kitchen immaculate. I could read the newspaper. But it was in the den. I couldn't go back there.

I could bake a cake! Jody Kline, cheery baker and kitchen worker. It would give me an excuse for staying in the kitchen, and when I was finished I could offer some to my father and Matt. Perhaps the aroma of a baking cake would even attract them to the kitchen. I took a spice cake mix from the shelf.

It was easy to throw all the ingredients together. As I stirred them I thought about my portrait of Matt in the closet upstairs. The real Jody Kline was in that picture, not in this cake I was making. But how could I hand that picture to him? He'd know I had been thinking about him, concentrating on him, spending time on him. This cake, on the other hand, was simple and innocent. Why is it that sometimes when you're eager to give more of yourself, you're forced to give less of yourself?

I poured the batter into a greased pan and stuck it in the oven. I would have a finished cake in about half an hour. Now what should I do? It isn't necessary to sit in a kitchen and guard an embryonic cake. Just set the oven timer and leave. I couldn't leave. So I just sat and tried to pick up snatches of conversation from the den.

My father and Matt were laughing. Was it time for a social hour? No. They were discussing a case, and apparently there was something humorous about it. It seemed so strange, so cozy, to have Matt right there in my house on a Sunday. Maybe his date with Tanya had ended early last night and that's why he was able to show up here fresh and ready for work. Keep that thought, Jody Kline.

The kitchen was beginning to smell nice. Would its aroma reach the den? I decided to make some fresh coffee to go with the cake. Now there would be the aromas of perking coffee and warm cake.

The timer went off. The cake was done. The voices continued in the den. What if my father and Matt stayed there for hours? And I was stuck in the kitchen for hours? I didn't want to be a domestic creature any longer. I wanted action.

I walked to the den. I couldn't smell the cake or the coffee there. My father and Matt were huddled together. "Would you two like some coffee and cake?" I asked.

I'd surprised them. I'd interrupted them. Matt looked at my father for a reaction.

"Sounds good," said my father, and he stretched.

"Okay, thanks," said Matt.

"In here or in the kitchen?" I asked.

"The kitchen," said my father. "We could use a change of scenery."

"Should we finish this page first?" asked Matt.

"No, we can pick it up. I know where we're at." My father stood up. Matt took a last look at a paper on the desk, and then he stood up.

They followed me into the kitchen. They sat down at the table. I was nervous cutting the cake, pouring the coffee, getting the cream and the sugar, and doing various hostess-type things while Matt watched me. I sat down at the table, opposite him.

"How have you been?" he asked as he poured cream into his coffee.

"Fine. Well, not so fine. I had to go, was literally *forced* to go, on this terrible date last night. I was fulfilling an obligation, and it was awful. Every minute of it was awful."

Why was I bringing up last night? I guess I was still

trying to explain to Matt why I broke the date with him. And now I had the additional information that I had done penance.

"That's too bad," he said, and he ate a piece of cake.

"The trials of youth," said my father.

I wasn't going to get any mileage out of last night's disaster. So I asked Matt, "How have *you* been?"

"Good. Busy. Your father's keeping me hopping." Matt grinned at my father. They were a compatible couple. If only Matt and I were! I wished the phone would ring and it would be for my father. If Matt and I were left alone, maybe we could work things out. Maybe he'd ask me out. Maybe I'd even get up enough nerve to show him the picture I'd drawn of him. My problems could all be settled over the kitchen table.

The telephone didn't ring. In fact, my father entered the conversation and dominated it. He talked about the case he and Matt were working on. I nodded, I smiled, I poured more coffee, I cut more pieces of cake, I stared at Matt. I examined every feature of his face. But this was more frustrating than not seeing him at all. When I didn't see him, I could at least *imagine* how wonderful it would be when I did see him. Some wonderful.

Suddenly my father excused himself. "I'll be back in a minute," he said. He went to the den. He probably had an idea he wanted to jot down. Sometimes he does that in the middle of a conversation. This was as good as a telephone call. Matt and I were alone.

Matt was sort of shoveling the crumbs of his cake with

his fork. It gave him an activity. "This is good cake," he said. "It's gingerbread, isn't it?"

"Spice."

Was he angry at me? I couldn't tell. He wanted to talk about cake. How about the future? This was his chance to ask me out again.

"Could I have another piece of cake?"

It was also his chance to ask me for another piece of cake.

I handed it to him. I felt like throwing it at him.

Suddenly he asked, "Do you like Australian movies?"

"Australian movies? You mean movies filmed in Australia or with a plot that takes place in Australia or both?"

I was asking questions I didn't want answered. I just wanted to know if he was inviting me to the movies.

"Both," he said. "There's one playing in the neighborhood and I—"

Matt stopped talking. My father had come back. "Coffee break over," he said without sitting down.

"I'll be right with you," Matt said, but he didn't move.

My father took the hint and went back to the den. Matt leaned across the table. "As I was saying, want to go to the movies with me when I'm finished here?"

That wasn't exactly what he'd been saying, but it was better.

"Sure." No point in hesitating or getting up to consult my calendar. We would be going out together, and soon!

Matt stood up. "I should be finished in an hour or so. Okay?"

"Terrific."

He went back to the den. I sat and stared blissfully at his crumbs. Finally I got up, put the food away, and went to my room. How should I spend this wonderful hour of anticipation? I felt exhilarated. I looked at R.E.'s sweater draped over the chair. I could rip it to pieces, unravel it, shred it, stomp on it, feed it to the garbage disposal piece by piece. Fantastic things could be done to this sweater. But I wasn't in the mood for destruction. I felt too happy. I would do something generous. I looked up Pete Summers's telephone number and dialed it.

He answered. "Pete Summers here."

"Hi, Pete," I said. "Is R.E. still around?"

"No, he left right after breakfast. But I'll be writing to him. Is there a message I can give him or is it"—Pete chuckled—"too private?"

"I've got his sweater and I want to return it. Could you mail it to him?"

"I guess so. How do you mail a sweater?"

"You just mail it like you'd mail any item of clothing. Haven't you ever mailed a birthday present or a Christmas present to someone?"

"My mom's the mailer in the family."

"Could I have R.E.'s address?"

"Sure. Why?"

"I'll mail the sweater."

Pete had the address memorized, including the zip code. After he gave it to me, he said, "Mailing's just not my thing. But my mom can do it."

"It's okay. I can do it," I said. The idea of personally dispatching the sweater appealed to me. Out of my room. Out of town. Gone.

I keep materials for mailing in my closet, because I send pictures to friends. I have a variety of sizes and shapes of envelopes. In the back of my closet were some large book bags. They probably weren't meant for sweaters, but I stuffed R.E.'s sweater into one anyway. It fitted, in a bulging sort of way. I wrote R.E.'s name and address with marking pen on the front of the package. For a return address I also wrote his name and address. I didn't want to see that sweater again. I would have to take the package to the post office tomorrow to get it weighed for the correct postage and mailed.

My sketchbook was in the front of the closet where I had placed it. I opened it and looked at Matt's picture. It looked finished, complete. I hardly ever complete a picture in one session. Even if I think I have, when I go back for another look I see that something is wrong. But this was another look, and the picture was right. As an artist, I was proud of it. I took it out of the closet and sat on my bed and stared at it. I wanted to share it. With Matt. I could give it to him today. No, it was too soon. I hardly knew him. He might wonder why I had been drawing his picture.

I put the picture on my bed and gazed at it while I changed my clothes.

Chapter 12

Matt wasn't finished in an hour. It was closer to two hours. By the time we were out of the house and into his car it was almost dinnertime. This was the night I was supposed to go out with my father for our weekly dinner. But my father got out of that nicely by saying he'd really rather stay home and eat a sandwich in front of the TV.

Matt started the car. "Movie first or dinner first?"

I shrugged.

"Okay, then, movie first. I think it starts soon, so we can see it from beginning to end."

The movie was boring. How could it be boring with Matt sitting beside me? Unfortunately there wasn't any transference of excitement from him to the screen. The movie was about some stranded settlers who kept exchanging long, significant looks. If you understood what the looks meant, you understood the movie. There was one big feast scene I understood. I was feeling hungry. I wished we had eaten first.

After the movie, as we were walking toward his car, Matt shook his head and said, "Dull, dull, dull."

"Don't stop," I said. "I thought it was worth at least two more dulls." We both laughed.

I couldn't believe the restaurant he picked out. Then I realized that he probably hadn't picked it out. It was the pretentious place my father had taken me to. My father had probably recommended it to Matt. However, this time as I was being seated in one of their silver-flecked, overdone, understated chairs, it all struck me as being romantic. It *was* romantic.

Now that I was in the restaurant, I didn't feel hungry. I just wanted to sit and stare at Matt across the table. But the waiter would have none of that. I ordered something.

After the waiter took our order, Matt said, "We're about twenty-four hours late."

"For what?"

"For going out together, of course. We were supposed to go out last night."

As if I could forget. I said, "Let's pretend tonight *is* last night."

"You really did have a miserable time?"

"Believe it. The worst. I shouldn't bring this up again but I feel so awkward about breaking that date with you."

"I'm afraid I didn't respond very graciously," said Matt. "I was surrounded by people and it was hard to talk. I think I was abrupt."

"No, you weren't abrupt. You were, well, sort of cool."

"Cool?" Matt laughed.

It was hard to connect him to that cold voice on the

phone. I had described it as cool, which was polite for cold.

"You should have seen what happened afterward," he said. "I had this extra ticket, right? I tried to give it away. It turned into a real hassle. If I had tried to sell it, I probably would have disposed of it in a flash."

"Go on," I said. I didn't want that to be the end. I had to know what he would say about Tanya Lipsert.

"Go on? Well, that's about it. Mr. Lipsert said that his daughter loved to go to plays. So I took her."

"Then what? Did you have a good time last night?"

He looked at me quizzically. "It was okay."

He didn't want to talk about it. I was dying to know what he thought of Tanya. As I sat there across the table from him, it was necessary for me to believe that Matt never wanted to see Tanya again. It was part of the total atmosphere.

"You look wonderful," Matt said suddenly.

"Well . . . I . . . thank you."

Always accept a compliment, Opal had told me. Never protest, never qualify it or undo it in any way. It's somebody's monument to you. Don't knock it down.

Matt took my hand. I hoped I wasn't falling in love. To be in love you should have a lot more to go on than I did. Think, Jody. Matt has yet to *call* you for a date. He ran into you at your father's office, he ran into you at your father's house. That's how your dates came about. They were always connected to your father. Caution, caution.

But Matt was looking at me as if he felt the same way I did.

The food came. "Did you ever finish the portrait of your maid's son?" he asked as the waiter left.

"Timmy's picture? You must be psychic. I finished it today. I'm presenting it tomorrow."

"What are you working on next?"

Here, handed to me, was a perfect chance to tell Matt about *his* picture. Should I? What would Opal do? Never mind. What would *I* do? Wait. "Maybe I'll show it to you sometime," I said.

"Who's the subject?"

"It's a secret."

"It's your dad, isn't it? I won't say anything."

"Is my dad working you hard?" I switched topics.

"It wouldn't be hard if I knew what I was doing. Your father's very patient with me."

"Maybe he's hoping to take you into the firm someday."

"You think so?" Matt's face seemed to light up. But he said, "I have college, I have law school. I have years of study ahead of me before that could happen."

Still, I could tell, he wanted it to happen.

I was sorry when dessert came. It signaled the end of the meal. I could order a second dessert. Childish. The rest of the evening picked up speed, as if accelerating toward a goal. But it was getting late, and Matt had a long trip home.

Too soon we were back in front of my house, in Matt's

car. "It was wonderful tonight," he said. He kissed me before I had a chance to think about whether he would. It was a long kiss. He liked me. I'd be seeing him again. I wasn't in any hurry to get out of the car. A week. Two weeks. No hurry.

"I hope your father won't be concerned that I kept you out so late," he said.

"I don't know what time it is and I don't care." I smiled and I settled into my seat.

"I do," Matt said. He opened his door, got out, and came around and opened my door. I got out. We started to walk up to my front door.

"Your father . . ." he said again.

"What about my father? Can't you think of me *separately?* First you were worried about your mother and my father, and now . . ." I stopped. What was I doing? I smiled again. A little forced. I had to keep this light. "Okay, I'm the boss's daughter. I get it. No sweat."

I had broken the mood. The date was over. And he didn't ask for another.

Chapter 13

Fortunately, my father was asleep, or at least in his room, when I got home, and he didn't poke his head out. Matt needn't have worried. I was the one who should worry. I had wrecked a beautiful evening. What I had demonically planned to do to R.E.'s sweater, I had done to my date with Matt.

Matt's picture was on my bed where I had left it. It was beside the bulging package that contained the sweater. Tomorrow the U.S. Postal Service would take the package off my hands. I started to put Matt's picture back in the closet. But I didn't. I stopped. I looked back at the package all ready to go out into the world, and I knew what I wanted to do with the picture. I would *mail* it to Matt. With a little note of apology for getting angry over nothing. Because that's exactly what I had done.

I got my drawing pencil and signed my name in a slant across the bottom right side of the picture. Then I got a pen and paper and wrote a note.

Dear Matt,

I hope you enjoy owning this picture I drew
of you. I'm sorry that

Somehow I couldn't *write* that I was sorry. If he had a
brain in his head he could tell I was, just by my sending
this picture. I rewrote the note.

Dear Matt,

I hope you enjoy owning this picture.

Sincerely,
Jody

He would know that I drew the picture, so there was no
point in mentioning it. It might sound as if I were brag-
ging. I put the picture in a mailer and added some extra
cardboards. I printed Matt's name on the front of the
package and addressed it in care of the law firm. I hoped
that no one else in the firm would notice my return
address, especially Mrs. Baxter.

I felt optimistic as I sealed the package. The picture
could speak better than I could. Matt would know how I
felt about him. I put the two packages on the chair. I
probably should have included a note for R.E., short and
polite, thanking him for lending me his sweater. Too late
now. I noted with satisfaction that the package for Matt
was neat and smooth.

Everything was in order, and I went to bed.

Chapter 14

I walked to the post office the next morning. The weather was warm but not hot. I was wearing shorts and a halter, and unlike Saturday night, I was dressed perfectly for the occasion. I mailed both packages first class. I was afraid they wouldn't accept the sweater package, but they did.

I decided to walk to Opal's apartment. I had nothing better to do, and besides, I was wondering how she was. I almost collided with her at her front door. She was dressed for work. "I'm going to the mall," she said. "Want to come?"

"Shopping?"

"Working."

"Are there doorbells in the mall?"

Opal smiled. "I don't always ring doorbells. Sometimes I stand on street corners or in malls. Today I have a supermarket survey to conduct in the mall."

"Is that like picking up strangers as they walk by?"

Before Opal could answer I said okay.

On the way to the mall in her car, she asked what decision I had made about breaking my date with Matt Green.

"There's good news and there's bad news, Opal," I said. "Wait a week and I'll tell you everything."

"There's an *everything?* Good," she said.

Inside the mall she stationed herself at an intersection. "This is a high-traffic spot," she said. "Thousands of shoppers will walk by here. Here I go." Opal went up to an elderly woman who was strolling by. "Isn't this a lovely day," Opal said.

The woman stopped and thought it over.

Opal wasn't waiting for an answer. She went on. "I'm doing a survey for area supermarkets, and we would welcome your valuable thoughts. Could I trouble you to answer a few questions?"

The woman appeared to be still working on the lovely day comment. But she seemed flattered by Opal's attention.

Opal asked, "Do you shop exclusively in one market?"

The woman liked the question. She opened up. "Well, yes, mostly I do, but then sometimes I don't. When my son-in-law buys my groceries for me, he goes to a different market from my regular, because he says the prices are cheaper. Even if they are, the cost of gas to drive to my son-in-law's market is—"

I signaled to Opal that I was leaving, and I mouthed, "I'll be back." Opal nodded.

I walked through the mall. I stopped and bought an

ice-cream cone. After I finished it I went into a record store. I didn't buy anything. I went into an art supplies store and bought three brushes. I went into the store where I had bought my yellow dress. If Betty couldn't clean mine, maybe I'd buy a duplicate. They had the dress in bright green only. It was bilious.

I started to walk back to Opal. Three girls passed me. Then they turned around, thinking they had recognized me. They had. One of the girls was Victoria, back too late from her camping trip in Maine. Tanya Lipsert was with her.

"Hi, Jody," said Victoria. "We're spending our summer in the mall. Whatcha been doin'?"

"Nothing much."

"Did you get someone for Saturday night?" Tanya asked.

"Yes."

"Fantastic. If you need anyone again, it would be best not to count on me. I may be tied up this summer."

"By whom?" asked the third girl, and she giggled. The third girl was Heather Rollins. She was in town, after all. What did I care now?

"This guy wouldn't tie me up," said Tanya. "That's against the law and he's very legal."

"So what's his name?" asked Victoria.

Tanya just smiled. She wasn't going to say anything else. Perhaps if Victoria pleaded, humbled herself . . .

Victoria wasn't really interested. She said to me, "Well, see you in the mall," and they walked away.

My mind was trying to sort things out. Tanya may or may not have known that I knew Matt. He wouldn't tell her that I had broken a date with him and that's why he had that extra ticket. Yet her legal remark seemed addressed to me. Unlike some other kids, Tanya never bragged about anything that didn't have some basis in fact. Matt must have at least asked her for another date. I was sorry I had mailed the picture.

I walked slowly, thinking. I had to get the picture back. But it was already mailed. You can't get something back once you mail it. Maybe Opal could! She could talk her way into and out of anything. I had recently seen several caper movies where the impossible was pulled off. But my package might already have left the post office. It was probably being transported by some cheerful employee of the postal service who would be astonished to learn he was the carrier of high embarrassment for Jody Kline. Forget the picture. It was too late.

I had lunch with Opal. I asked her if she had ever done a survey for the U.S. Postal Service. What did it cost me to ask. Maybe she had a friend there. She could make a phone call. Opal had no friends in the post office, and she was trying to concentrate on her supermarket stuff. While she ate, she went over the interviews she had completed. After lunch I stuck around and observed her in action. It was amazing how some of the people she stopped were good-natured and went on and on in their responses as if this were the highlight of their day. Other people were rude, and someone told her to stop loitering or he'd call the police.

At four thirty she said, "That's it for today."

We walked to Opal's car. "How did it go?" I asked. "I couldn't tell."

"Very well. Two more days of this and the project will be completed."

"Isn't it tiring to stand on your feet all that time and talk?"

"Not while I'm doing it. Afterward it's tiring. When it hits me that I've done it."

Opal started the motor and we drove off. "So now you have to go home and prepare supper for yourself?" I asked.

"Unfortunately. I wish I had developed a taste for TV dinners."

"Have dinner with us. At my house."

"You cook for me? Don't be ridiculous."

"We have a maid who cooks. She'll just set a place for one more. Nothing fancy. There'll only be my father and me. *Please.*"

I didn't mind saying please to Opal Spiegel. She had cooked that nice lunch for me at her house, and if fate had decreed that she was to meet my father tonight over Betty's roast beef, well, what could I do?

"Give me time to nap and change my clothes," she said.

Chapter 15

My father's eyes almost popped out of his head when he saw Opal Spiegel. So did mine, for different reasons. He had expected "my friend Opal" to be a teenager. I had told him that I invited a friend to dinner. I gave him as little information about Opal as he had given me about Gossamer and Matt Green. My shock was based on Opal's changed appearance. She couldn't have spent any time taking a nap before she arrived. She must have gone someplace to get herself done over. How had she managed it? In about two hours her hair had grown longer, her body had grown slimmer, her face had grown younger. To top everything off, her electric-blue dress had sound effects when she moved. Swish-crackle.

Betty was third in line to be surprised. She had also thought that my friend would be a teenager. Betty glanced at my father as if he could unravel the mystery. My father pretended there wasn't any mystery. He and Opal and I sat around the living room waiting for dinner to be ready. Opal selected the same chair she had sat in when she came to my house for her deodorant cans interview. My father was about to ask her some questions, but Opal got there first. "Jody tells me you're an attorney."

"Yes."

"In New York City."

"Yes."

"It must be stimulating work."

"Sometimes."

What was happening? Opal was treating my father as if he were the subject of a market research interview. I spoke up. "Opal is a writer in her spare time. You should see some of her works."

"Oh, isn't that interesting," my father said. "What kind of writing do you do?"

"Fragments. I specialize in fragments."

"I'm afraid I'm not familiar with that. Is it a recognized literary form?"

"It's whatever comes into my mind that should be written down. Short pieces usually, with no beginning or end. They're just there."

"Just there?" My father was puzzled.

"Yes. Unconnected. No plots. No characters."

My father poured himself a drink. He offered one to Opal, but she declined. I knew he was wishing that Opal were a teenager. He never knew what they were talking about, either, but that was okay.

Opal resumed questioning my father. I butted in to inform my father that Opal was a market researcher. I hoped that would make her seem professional rather than nosy.

My father managed to get in a question. "How did you two meet?"

It was a fatherly question. I had picked up this middle-aged friend somewhere, somehow. What had I been doing with my summer? Why hadn't he kept better track of me!

"I rang your doorbell and she let me in," said Opal. "She was a very lovely interviewee."

Wonderful. Just wonderful. My father would probably never let me out of his sight again. He was speechless.

Over dinner he regained his speech. He made polite conversation with Opal. But there wasn't any spark in it. He wasn't interested in Opal as a woman. Was she interested in him as a man? She got all fixed up to meet him. It would be so great if he asked her out. Just once. It would break the Gossamer habit.

By the time Betty served dessert, Opal and my father were getting along better. Opal quoted one of her better fragments and my father seemed impressed. She told him some anecdotes about her work, and his laugh was genuine.

Betty went home after dinner. Opal, my father, and I stayed at the table, relaxed and full. I was congratulating myself on having arranged this meeting. Opal had not been pushy, and my father had not been too upper-class. They were getting along.

Opal looked at her watch. "This was delightful," she said. "But I must be going soon."

"Stay," I said.

My father nodded.

"I've already told someone to pick me up here," said Opal.

"Pick you up?" I asked. "Didn't you drive over?"

"I walked. Didn't you notice that there was no car in front when you opened the door to let me in?"

"No, I only noticed you." A simple no would have answered her question better.

Shortly after nine our doorbell rang. I answered it. A man was standing there. He looked like a TV spokesman for expensive foreign cars. In a way, he looked richer than my father. "Is Opal Spiegel here?" he asked in a deep voice.

Opal was on her way to the door. "Carl," she said to the man. She kissed him on the cheek. "I'd like you to meet Jody Kline and her father, Gerald. Carl Stamp."

"A pleasure," the man said, extending his hand. He was smooth. He was Opal's boyfriend. That was obvious. She had more going on in her life than I had thought. She wasn't available for my father. She hadn't gotten dressed up for my father. It was for this Carl.

After they left, my father said, "Nice try, Jody."

"What do you mean?"

"You know."

My father seemed more amused than mad. But he went on. "It's not wise to make friends with strangers who ring your doorbell. Have you asked yourself why you cultivated this relationship? I think you're hungry for a mother."

"I'm not!"

"I won't press the issue, but think about it. Gossamer has her faults, but people settle in after a while to their new roles, and they rise to fit them."

"Gossamer? New role?" My father had turned the evening around into a selling point for his marrying Gossamer Green. He was a lawyer rearranging facts to favor his own position. But I didn't want to fight with him.

"Let's drop it," I said. "But I'm still going to be friends with Opal."

"Fine. She's rather a fascinating person."

"She is?"

"Certainly. How could you miss it?"

"Well, I thought *you* could miss it. But I'm glad you didn't."

I went into the kitchen and straightened up a bit. Then I went to bed. I will never know if my father would have asked Opal out if Carl hadn't shown up. I will never know if Opal would have said yes. The name Carl Stamp stayed in my mind. There are Carl Stamps in the shadows everywhere. They're the persons who are destined to screw up your plans simply because you are unaware they exist. Innocently they go about their own activities, selling foreign cars on TV, or however they pass the time, until they pop up in your life as a fully developed disaster. I wished a Carl Stamp on Gossamer Green. I wished a Carl Stamp on Tanya Lipsert. It helped me fall asleep.

Chapter 16

I painted nine pictures during the next three weeks. I plunged into my work by romanticizing myself as a luckless artist whose only salvation lay in her art. I sat in my backyard and painted pictures of trees and fences and grass. I painted a picture of the back of my house. I added people and animals coming and going. That was the most fun and the hardest work, creating things that weren't there.

I tried not to watch for the mail or pay attention to the telephone. I had made a mental list of the three ways Matt would respond to my picture:

1. by mail, because that was how he had received it.
2. by telephone, because it's easier.
3. not at all.

One day when I was at the supermarket, a guy called me. When I got home, Betty mentioned it matter-of-factly. "Didn't he leave his name?" I asked. "What did he say? Did he say he'd call back? What was his voice like? What kind of background noises could you hear?"

Poor Betty was perplexed. "Well, he had a nice voice. He hesitated when I asked for his name, but he didn't give it. He said he'd call back. He didn't say when. He was polite. Background noises? I couldn't hear traffic or bells or machinery going. Nothing. This was an important call, huh?"

"Probably not."

"If he calls again, and you're not here, I won't let him get away. I'll get his life story, Jody."

"That's okay, Betty."

I shrugged off the call. It could have been anyone. Really, why would Matt call? He had never called on his own. Besides, I had broken a date with him, ended another one on a sour note, and he had found Tanya Lipsert. That was that. I wondered what he had done with the picture. Would he keep it in sight or hide it? Would he destroy it? To me it was a sin to destroy someone's artwork.

The telephone rings at random, so there was no point in sitting around waiting for the guy to call back. That's what I told myself as I sat around anyway for the next few days, hoping I'd hear from him again. I didn't.

The delivery of the mail, however, wasn't random. I was aware of the arrival of the mailman each day. I got an education in how truly boring mail can be. Everything that had an envelope with the address behind a little plastic window was boring. So was metered mail. Usually rectangular-shaped mail was boring, although that was the shape of most envelopes. Mail addressed to OCCU-PANT was boring. I also learned that there is something ominously dependable about most of the mail. The electric company won't forget you, your dentist won't forget you, the sweepstakes people won't forget you. Only Matt Green will forget you.

Almost three weeks after I mailed out the picture to Matt, a little square envelope with my name and address scrawled across the front arrived. There was no return address. Suddenly I realized how much I had yearned for this letter from Matt. Matt had terrible handwriting, and I loved it. I turned the envelope over to open it. There was a name and address on the back. The name was R. E. Cross.

R. E. Cross! For a moment I couldn't understand why he was writing to me. Then I remembered. I had mailed his sweater to him the same day I mailed the picture to Matt. The envelope lost its magic. I opened it.

Dear Jody,

Is Jody spelled with an *i* or a *y?* I forgot to ask Pete. Also, are you Kline or Klein?

I'm writing to thank you for sending my sweater. Sombody else might have thrown it away or kept it. It's my favorite sweater. I also want to thank you for packing it so well. It arrived in good shape.

I enjoyed meeting you. Pete and I got
carried away with our camp stories and it
wasn't too interesting for you, I bet. I hope
to see you again, and no camp stories.

Sincerely,

R. E. Cross

P.S. I would have written sooner, but I had
to get your address from Pete.

The short letter was better than the entire date with
R. E. Cross. He wasn't so bad after all. It made me feel
better about the date, but not much better. His polite
note made the lack of a note from Matt seem worse than
before. Just to be *polite*, Matt should have written.

The telephone rang. Wouldn't it be nicely coincidental
if that were Matt calling? It wasn't. It was Alison, crying.
"I wanted to call you last night," she said. "But I thought
you wouldn't be up at midnight."

"What's wrong, Alison?"

"Pete and I have broken up. That is, he broke up with
me."

"Impossible."

"No, it isn't. It happened." Alison kept crying.

"Want me to come over? Or do you want to come over
here?"

"I'll come over. Is Betty there? I don't want her to
know."

"Just come over. We can talk in the yard. I've been out there painting. I'll make some lemonade and we'll talk."

"Lemonade? Is that some kind of therapy? I just want to talk."

Alison came over an hour later. "I kept washing my face for the trip, but then I'd cry again," she said.

We sat out in the yard. Alison gulped down the lemonade I had made. "Well, it's all very simple," she said. "Last night Pete said that we should date other people. That we've been going steady forever and it cuts us off from having other experiences. Other experiences! I didn't ask him what he meant by that. I wonder who he met."

"You mean another girl?"

"Sure. Why else would he dump me? I'm devastated."

I had a little problem with this conversation. Alison didn't know that I thought Pete Summers was a jerk. I had hoped for a long time that they would break up. Alison had just handed me the best news I'd had in weeks.

"Alison, you won't believe this now, but you'll be happy in the future that this happened."

"What?" She made a face. "That's the kind of dumb advice I'd expect to hear from someone over thirty. Where do you get off saying that?"

"Okay, here goes. Remember the night we doubledated? You were so blind about Pete that you didn't even realize he was ignoring you. It was a hideous evening."

"I thought you had a good time."

"Rotten time. But I didn't want to make waves. I just got a note from R.E., and even he knew that they shut us out. It took him a while, but he knew."

"Well, the guys hadn't seen each other for ages, that was all. Have you seen Pete around with any girl? Tell me the truth. I have to know."

"I never see Pete. Only at school. Or at your house sometimes."

Alison started to wail. "At my house. That might never happen again. It's part of my past. Now it's my nostalgia and my heartbreak."

"Come off it, Alison. Don't you ever look at other guys? Don't you ever want a little *variety* in your life? Isn't there *anybody* besides Pete that you've wanted to go out with?"

"No."

"Well, there should be. Pete might change his mind and want to resume with you. But I wouldn't jump back into it."

"You think he'd change his mind?"

"Maybe."

"You've given me hope."

"Alison, don't say that. This is your chance to get *away* from Pete."

Alison stopped crying. She looked at me suspiciously. "You've got a crush on Pete, haven't you?"

Alison was not an A-student at school or an A-student in real life.

"No. *No!*" I said.

"Maybe you have and you don't know it. It could be subliminal."

"If I discover it, I'll let you know."

Alison looked around. Her mood was changing. She started to admire my paintings. In the midst of it she said, "I'm a better person than Pete. I really am."

"Congratulations on your discovery."

She remembered me. "Have you heard from Matt since your movie date?"

I had told her about Matt's Sunday visit to my house. But she didn't know about the picture. Nobody knew about the picture. She didn't know how far to the bottom I had sunk.

"Haven't heard anything. But I'm not moping around. I've been productive."

"Losing yourself in your work, huh?"

"I'd be doing this anyway. This was how I had planned to spend my summer."

"Maybe I need a hobby."

"This isn't a hobby. This is my—"

"Soul? Yeah, that's what I need. Something to nourish my soul. Maybe I'll take up painting."

"They need volunteers to paint the recreation room at the youth center."

"Not that kind of painting."

"Don't put it down. It's a summer project, and you'd be with a bunch of kids who also volunteered to help."

"You mean boys. You want me to be with other boys."

"Boys, girls, anybody who volunteers."

"Is this therapy? I don't believe in therapy." Alison gazed into her empty lemonade glass. Then she put it down. "I only drank it because I was thirsty. I'll only paint walls if *I* want to."

Alison spent the rest of the day with me. She went home in much better condition than she had been in when she arrived. As far as I was concerned, the day had been a celebration in honor of Pete Summers leaving her life.

But it wasn't that easy. The next day Alsion latched on to someone to take Pete's place. Me. She called me. "I'm going to the youth center, and I want you to go with me."

"Why?"

"I just don't want to go alone."

"Okay. But I won't stay."

I knew some of the kids who were involved in the rec room project. One of them was Tanya Lipsert. She was known for her volunteer work as well as for her slogan, "Privileged people owe something to the rest of the world." Tanya would cringe if she knew I called it a slogan, but what else was it when she repeated it so often? The rec room project did not involve the rest of the world. It was for high school kids in the community, and of course that included Tanya.

The rec room was almost deserted when Alison and I arrived. It was partially painted. Some of it was bright tan, some of it was dull tan. The project was to replace tan with tan. Kids can get discouraged doing that. I've never painted graphics, but I felt like volunteering to jazz up the walls with a lively design.

Linda Zalt and Amy Vincetti were mixing paint. Tanya wasn't there. "The rescue team," Linda said when she saw us. "Now Amy and I won't have to finish this miserable job all by ourselves."

Alison nudged me. "A bunch of kids, you said. Some bunch of kids. Exactly two. And one of them is Amy Vincetti. She's been after Pete for years. This I don't need."

Alison and I started to walk out.

"Girls!" Someone was calling to us. It was Ms. Marker, head of student volunteers. She never let anyone escape. She took control of my summer.

Chapter 17

Ms. Marker was interviewing us. "We never take any-one on without an interview," she explained.

Her office was a cubicle near the rec room. It was decorated with posters from the government. She wrote down our names, addresses, telephone numbers, and ages. Then she asked about our experience and inter-ests.

"I like to paint," I said, biting my tongue the moment I said it.

"Well, you've come to the right place," she said.

Ms. Marker smiled. When she smiled you could see that her group had 85 percent fewer cavities. That's one of the reasons she was hired. Her background was public relations. She did a variety of jobs for the school system, and she always made them sound more interesting and more valuable than they were. Her summer title was Director of Student Volunteers for Summer Projects.

When Ms. Marker looked at you, it was usually at a spot just over your head, as if you had something fasci-nating perched there. She looked up at me and then wrote, "Jody Kline, painter," saying the words as she wrote them. She said them with the pride of someone who had read a thick book and extracted its essence. I wasn't anybody's daughter, anybody's friend, I wasn't an A-student, I wasn't a French cook, I wasn't even someone who had picked the wrong guy to like.

She turned to Alison, who was squirming. The cubicle was hot and getting hotter. Ms. Marker was wearing a suit that you would expect to see on someone in midwinter. She looked completely cool. People who conquer the weather terrify me. "And what do you do, dear?" she asked Alison.

Alison was smart. "Not much," she said. "Hardly anything. No skills."

Terrific! If Alison escaped, I could escape too.

"Everyone does something," said Ms. Marker.

Alison shrugged. "I guess I'm an exception."

Bless and keep from harm all the days of her life my friend Alison August.

Alison went on. "I kind of get up in the morning and say, 'Hello, Sun.' And of course the sun doesn't answer me, and I feel absolutely rejected. The sun not answering me is a real turnoff, and so I don't do anything but mope around the rest of the day."

I tried to warn Alison with my eyes. She was going too far. Trying to present yourself as a weirdo when you're not takes immense talent.

"You're very articulate and lyrical," said Ms. Marker. "Tell me more."

Alison obliged by telling Ms. Marker more and more things she couldn't do.

All of Alison's failings were redefined by Ms. Marker and emerged as assets.

Ms. Marker told us that she had work for both of us. But before she told us what it was, she gave a spiel of how heartwarming it was that we came to volunteer. She reeled off her speech like you hear police officers on TV monotonously recite, "You have the right to remain silent." Somewhere she must own a card with that speech printed out.

"Now," she said, "I have something that's not demanding and not *un*demanding. That's what we want in these hot summer months, right?"

Months? How long would this be going on?

"This is a real plum, and you can start immediately." Ms. Marker looked at the clock on the wall. "In fact, you have several working hours left today!" She almost quivered with excitement. She had discovered gold in an unexpected place. It was Sutter's Mill all over again. Brace yourself for the stampede west.

"I'm painting walls, right?" I asked.

"No. You did come to the right place for that, but as you can see we're not making much progress out there. The father of one of our students is a professional house painter. He promised to finish the room for us."

"Well, that's what we really came to do, Ms. Marker," I said. "That's all I know. Painting. And Alison, well, she's a washout in everything."

Alison nodded enthusiastically.

Ms. Marker turned grim. "I don't understand you young people. There's such a *need* out there. And you have time on your hands."

"Maybe a small project," I said.

"Well, what did you think I had in mind for you? It *is* a small project. Small cans. I'd like you two to collect cans for our food drive. Usually it's done around Thanksgiving, but people have a tendency to forget the hungry in the summer. So the need is almost greater now."

Alison shrugged. "I guess we could do that. Yeah, we'll do that."

"Fine," said Ms. Marker. "I'll give you an area that's near your homes. You'll work as a pair. We don't want you ringing doorbells alone."

Ringing doorbells! I was in Opal Spiegel's business. She was taking people's time. I was taking their cans.

Ms. Marker gave us an education in collecting cans. There was more to it than a person might think. She took out a map of our neighborhood. She was really prepared. She sectioned off an area with a pencil. It looked small on the map. But it was tremendous when you had to go door to door.

"That could take us all summer," said Alison, revealing that she had a talent for reading maps.

"Two or three hours a day and you can wind it up before school resumes," said Ms. Marker. "If you have a supermarket-type shopping cart, it would speed up your collections. They're excellent for transporting cans."

"But we'd have to go back to our houses over and over to empty the wagon and and then start up again," said Alison, revealing still another talent in projection and planning.

"Walking is the best exercise of all," said Ms. Marker.

"Not that much," said Alison. "Jody and I will do half the route."

"Three fourths," said Ms. Marker.

"Two thirds," said Alison, now revealing ability in both negotiation and math.

"Agreed," said Ms. Marker, and she sectioned off the map again. "When you're finished, another volunteer will come by your houses to pick up the cans in a truck. Thank you again for volunteering."

On the way home, Alison asked, "Did she take advantage of us?"

"Yes."

"We let her?"

"You put up a good fight. And, anyway, she appealed to our charitable instincts."

"She didn't appeal to me at all," said Alison. And she grinned.

"Alison, you're feeling better."

"No, I'm not. When I saw Amy Vincetti in the rec room I realized how many girls will be after Pete now. Amy is a symbol."

Alison sighed, and I let it go at that.

At home the mail had arrived. "Something crazy for you in the mail," said Betty. "It was returned. It has your name and return address on it."

Betty was sitting at the kitchen table. Behind her, taped to the refrigerator, was my picture of Timmy.

When I had given it to her, she was thrilled. She had shown it to Timmy and kept repeating, "You, you." Then, as she did with the pictures Timmy drew in school in his expert six-year-old style, she had taped it to the refrigerator. That was the place of honor for the pictures in Betty's life, I guess.

My "crazy" mail was on the table. I picked it up. It was a package addressed to Matt Green. It was all banged up, and it looked as if someone had chewed through it. It had post office messages stamped on it. NOT AT THIS ADDRESS. RETURN TO SENDER. Matt had never received his picture! Who had sent it back? I'd probably never know. Maybe it was one of the substitutes the law firm uses when Mrs. Baxter is on vacation. She takes erratic vacations. Three days here, four days there. This was good news. Matt had never received the picture, and that's why he hadn't thanked me for it.

Betty looked at me curiously. I said, "A shark got it." Then I waved the package as if it were something humorous, and I left the kitchen. I went to my room and opened the package. The picture had two diagonal folds through it. I couldn't send out a picture with two diagonal folds through it. I wasn't going to anyway. Getting the picture back was my reprieve. But as I looked at it, with its two diagonal folds, I wondered what benevolent forces in the U.S. Postal Service had watched over the bulging package containing R. E. Cross's sweater and delivered it over one thousand miles away without, as the saying goes, dropping a stitch.

I put the picture in my closet.

Chapter 18

I thought about Matt Green for the rest of the day. I had nothing going with him at all. There was nothing to expect from him, nothing to look forward to, nothing to dream about. Now that the picture was back, I realized how much thinking about it had kept me going.

Night came, and I was still thinking about him. Should I call him? I was back to that idea. I wanted to hear his voice. We could talk. Hearing my voice, he'd know that I wasn't mad at him. He'd remember how great most of our date had been. He might even compare me to the way Tanya sounds over the telephone. Her voice sounds like metal.

I looked up Matt's telephone number again. I dialed it. Someone answered quickly. On the first ring. I was so nervous I thought I'd pass out.

"Clarice's Clip Joint." It was a female voice.

"What?"

"Clarice's Clip Joint."

"This isn't the Green residence?"

"No, this is a dog-grooming salon."

"Sorry." I hung up.

Rats! I had dialed the wrong number. I probably would have been talking to Matt right now if I hadn't dialed a three instead of a two, or a five instead of a six, or whatever number I had dialed incorrectly.

I'd have to try again. I looked up Clarice's Clip Joint in the telephone book. I wanted to be very careful that I didn't dial that number again. I stared at the number. I couldn't believe it. I had made *three* mistakes! I had dialed a five instead of a six, a nine instead of an eight, and another nine instead of an eight. My confidence was gone. My plan was gone. It wasn't meant to be.

I called Opal. I was careful how I dialed. My one-week report to her on Matt was long overdue. I thought she'd be nagging me for it. But she had called to thank me for the dinner at my house, and she hadn't called again. She was probably busy with Carl. I felt less close to her after I met Carl. She had a whole other life she hadn't told me about. But she didn't owe me an explanation.

There wasn't any answer at Opal's. I'd try again sometime. My bad news could wait.

Chapter 19

Collecting cans was a drag and a pleasure. The drag part was the actual collecting. The pleasure was knowing that the contents of the cans would feed hungry stomachs. Alison and I were conscientious. We had accepted the job and we were carrying it out. Usually we tried to go early in the morning before it got hot, or late in the day when it had cooled off but wasn't yet dark. Alison's family owned a shopping cart, and we used it. I hoped it would last the summer. The cans did a job on it.

At first, I was afraid that doors would slam in our faces. But most people were kind and generous. There were a few houses we didn't want to approach. Some of them had legends connected to them. A witch lives here, a weirdo lives there, this man throws water on people who ring his bell. I had collected this information since childhood, and I didn't believe most of it. I certainly didn't believe the witch story. The man with the water, well, it was a possibility. In all, there were about seven houses we avoided. Houses without legends that we didn't want to approach were Amy Vincetti's, Pete Summers's, and Tanya Lipsert's. Alison was afraid that Amy would tell her something she didn't want to hear. As for Pete, Alison said, "Me go up and ring his bell? I'm not that crazy!" I had told Alison that Matt had used my ticket for Tanya and that I did not want to go to her house. Alison agreed. "You have one untouchable house, and I have two," she said.

We had to walk by Tanya's house. "Walk fast," I said. But we were pulling lots of cans in our wagon. I saw Tanya's mother. She was in front of her house, gardening. Mrs. Lipsert is an intellectual with a nervous tic that probably comes from too much thinking or too much energy. However, she's a lovely lady. Genuine. She spotted us. "Collecting cans?" she asked. "Stay right there. I'll get some."

Mrs. Lipsert dashed into her house and came out with an armload of cans. She carefully placed them in our wagon. "If cans are damaged, people might fear botulism and throw them out," she warned us.

My life was always a little improved when I saw Mrs. Lipsert. I picked up something of interest each time. It must be great for Mr. Lipsert to be married to someone so knowledgeable. Even though he's a partner in this prestigious law firm, and Mrs. Lipsert stays home and gardens and joins clubs, everyone knows she's ten times smarter than he is.

She put her arm around me affectionately, and I didn't mind. I knew she meant it. Suddenly I ached for a mother like her. I ached for a mother.

"How've you been, Jody?" she asked.

"Okay, I guess."

"And your dad? I saw him the last time I was at the office. He's looking well."

"I suppose so. I see him all the time, so I don't notice."

"You girls are doing a fine thing, collecting these cans. But wouldn't it be easier if you had two wagons?"

Without waiting for an answer Mrs. Lipsert once again dashed into her house and came back rolling a shopping wagon. "Here," she said. "This has been gathering dust in my basement. If it gets damaged, don't worry about it. We haven't used it in years."

"Thank you, Mrs. Lipsert," said Alison. "We appreciate it."

"A lot," I said. I kissed Mrs. Lipsert on the cheek. I had never before kissed her, but it seemed like a natural thing to do. Tanya came out of the house. Maybe she had been watching from the window. "Stealing my mother?" she asked.

I hated Tanya. Right then and there. I hadn't hated her before. There were her little angles and poses that had annoyed me, and her veiled references to Matt. But this was a direct blow. I didn't have a mother. She did.

Mrs. Lipsert squeezed me, as if to reassure me. She didn't say anything to Tanya, at least not in front of me. This very smart lady probably knew she got a lemon when she got Tanya. Maybe she was yearning for a daughter like me as much as I was yearning for a mother.

Alison and I walked on. There were tears in my eyes. I hoped nobody saw them. It was the second time this summer I had cried. Once over Matt Green, and now over my mother. Two people who were out of my life.

Chapter 20

We received an invitation to the Winklemans' annual summer lawn party. Mr. and Mrs. Winkleman invite everyone at Winkleman, Hackett, Lipsert, Ives, Kline & Bradford and their families to this yearly event that takes place under a tremendous tent in their tremendous backyard at tremendous expense. I like those parties. They make me feel like English royalty, privileged and elegant. Nothing I'd want to feel for very long, but it's great for an afternoon.

This year, though, there would be a problem. Matt Green would probably be there with Tanya Lipsert. I refused to let that keep me away. The party was three weeks into the future, anyway, toward the end of the summer. Summer coming to an end! What had I accomplished? Some of the best drawings and paintings I'd ever done. And, in a way, I'd helped to feed hungry people. That job wasn't over yet. Alison and I had four more streets to cover.

When my father got home and saw the invitation, he

assumed I'd be going to the party. It dawned on me that he'd be taking Gossamer.

"Are you taking Gossamer to it?" I asked.

"Yes, but I want you to come too."

"The three of us?"

"The three of us."

"Okay."

I was trying to accept Gossamer. For my father's sake. If I just gave her half a chance, I would probably find some good qualities in her. Matt obviously loved her. She must have done something to inspire it. Matt! I would see him again. So what? The U.S. Postal Service and Clarice's Clip Joint had conspired to keep me from making a fool of myself over him. I was not going to undo their good work.

Between the cans and my artwork, the days had been going by. I almost forgot about Opal. I had tried calling her two more times, but there still wasn't any answer. I thought about walking to her place someday, but I was tired of walking. Ms. Marker had said it was the best exercise. Maybe it was if you did it on a smooth path under cool leaves and possibly by a rippling brook. Lugging shopping wagons full of cans up and down hilly streets is not the best of anything.

Alison and I decided to finish the job in one day, a kind of can marathon. We covered our territory quickly. It was like a last spurt, and the finish line was in sight. At last we were done. "Finished!" I said to Alison. "We're free, free, free. Let's go home."

Alison didn't move. "Let's do one more," she said.

"Where? Are you crazy? Didn't you hear me say the most beautiful word in the English language, *finished?*"

"We didn't go to Pete's house."

"You didn't just say 'Pete's house'?"

"Yes. I have a right, a duty, to collect cans at his house. It's part of our designated route."

"Changed your mind, huh? You were avoiding his house."

"Another can is another can," said Alison.

"Have you heard from him since you broke up?"

"No."

"Let it drop, Alison."

"I want to collect cans from Pete."

We dragged our wagons to Pete's house. We both walked up his front steps. His parents worked, so there was a good chance that if the door opened, Pete would be there. Alison rang the bell. The door opened after a fairly long wait. Amy Vincetti was there. I was happy to see that she was fully clothed.

Alison looked at her in shock. She almost turned and ran, I could tell. But I said, "Hello, Amy. Is Pete home? We're collecting cans for the needy."

"Just a minute. I'll tell Pete you're here."

Amy left us standing at the door.

Alison said, "You were right. I'm so dumb. I'm myopic. Pete's an idiot and I should have seen through him. That does it. We're all through!"

Alison turned and ran down the stairs. Then she ran down the street, leaving me with the two shopping carts.

Pete came to the door. "We're collecting cans," I said. "Well, anyway, I'm collecting cans."

"Isn't Alison with you? Amy said Alison was with you."

"She had to leave."

Pete waited for me to say more, but I didn't. He invited me in. I was surprised, but I went. I left two unguarded shopping carts full of cans on the street. If anyone took them, they couldn't make a quick escape.

Pete led me down to his basement. There were five kids there, including Amy! "My folks just got this home computer, and I'm inviting everyone over to see it," he said. "I called Alison, but there wasn't any answer."

"We've been out collecting cans."

"I wanted to talk to Alison about more than computers. I miss her. I was out of my skull to let her go. I want to get back together again. You're her best friend, so I guess I can tell you that."

"Yes, you can tell me that," I said.

"I've been trying to get up enough nerve to call her. Would you tell her that I want to call her . . . kind of smooth my path? She just ran away from me, didn't she? She was at my door and she ran away. Please fix things up for us."

"Okay."

I watched Pete while he demonstrated marvelous things his computer could do. I would have to tell Alison that Pete wasn't having a private party with Amy. I would have to tell her that he was itching to get back together with her.

I left Pete's house with three cans of baked beans. My shopping wagons were still outside. I saw Alison waiting for me at the next corner. I would tell her what had happened and what hadn't happened. I would tell her that Pete wanted to go back to the way they were. Alison and Pete would be together again.

Alison's future as Mrs. Pete Summers appeared before me. They would get married at a young age, probably right after high school graduation. They would brag to everybody that neither of them had ever dated anyone else. Pristine and almost holy, they would be "the childhood sweethearts." Alison would settle in fast. She would have three babies in a row. She would wear dumpy housedresses to accommodate her increasingly dumpy figure. She would be the first in our group to get varicose veins. She would sit at the kitchen table in her twilight zone, endlessly clipping supermarket coupons and exulting over a special on mayonnaise.

I reached Alison. She looked at me expectantly. "Well?"

"I think they were making out on the couch," I said.

Chapter 21

Five days had passed since I had lied to Alison. The lie got bigger each day, not because I added to it, but because I just let it be. Why had I done it? Just because *I* thought Pete was a jerk? Alison had a right to go out with and marry a jerk. She had a right to live in the twilight zone of mayonnaise specials. Who was I to make decisions for her? I was so sorry for what I had done. But how could I confess? I had betrayed our friendship. There was no excuse I could make to her or to myself.

My father noticed that I was moping around the house. "Is there something bothering you?" he asked.

"Yes."

"It must be important."

"Very. It has to do with what kind of person I am. Like, am I a liar?" I started to cry. What was wrong with me this summer? Crying and lying. They rhymed . . . very funny.

"If you want to confide in me, Jody, well, I'm on *your* side, whatever it is. And it couldn't be all that bad."

My father was surprisingly gentle. He felt very strongly about lying, that it was almost a sin. As a lawyer he never lied, he just twisted the truth like crazy. I guess they're allowed to do that.

He seemed anxious for me to confide in him. I needed to confide in somebody. But I had never confided in my father about Matt. I hadn't told him about my friendship with Opal until he had actually met her. Maybe I thought he wasn't anybody to tell anything to.

"I'm on your side," he said again. "I know that sometimes our talks end in a disagreement, but that's not so serious, is it?"

"I guess not."

"Actually, it's healthy, it's honest. Silence can be unhealthy. So?"

I told my father about my lie.

He let out a low whistle. "I see what you mean. It was a whopper."

"Yeah."

My father pointed to the telephone. "Call Alison now and tell her. Get it over with."

"How about in an hour? So I can rehearse."

"That hour is going to turn into two hours," he said. "Which will turn into four hours. Ever hear of the expression now or never? It has merit."

"What should I say to her?"

"Whatever feels right to you."

"Oh, Daddy." I hugged him. I also called him Daddy. I think he noticed.

Alison's mother answered the phone. She got Alison.

"Alison, it's me. I've got something to tell you. Listen."

"What do you think I'm going to do—not listen? I hope you're not going to sock me with more bad news."

"Well, the other day I turned good news into bad news for you. I lied to you about Pete and Amy. Pete had five kids in his house when I went in. *Five* kids. His family got a computer and he was showing it off. He was *not* alone with Amy. In addition—now listen carefully—he told me he was out of his skull—his exact words—to let you go. He wants to get back together again, and he'd been trying to get up enough nerve to call you. He finally did call to ask you over to see the computer, but there was no answer. He asked me to tell you all of this, to fix things up so you two could get back together again. And, oh, yes, he said he missed you."

Something inside me hoped that since I was the bearer of such good news in such great detail, I would be treated warmly as a messenger of glad tidings.

"You rat!" said Alison. "Is this the truth? Tell me, is this the truth?"

"The whole truth."

Alison calmed down. "No, it isn't. You're making it up because you think I'm suicidal or something."

"I wish I were making it up."

"You wish you were!" Alison was excited again. "How could you wish that?"

"Because I wanted you and Pete to stay apart. I wanted you to go out with other guys. That's why I did it."

"But I don't want to go out with other guys."

"I know that now. Finally it's gotten home to me."

"Let's back up. Pete *really* wants to get back together with me?"

"That's what he told me."

Alison started to scream. "He loves me! He loves me!"

Then there was a silence I'll never forget, followed by "You *lied* to me! How could you?" Alison slammed down the receiver.

I went back to my father. "She hung up on me."

"You had to expect that."

"I know it. But it was awful. Do you think she'll ever forgive me?"

"Yes, definitely. Alison doesn't hold grudges for very long."

"But do you think she'll ever trust me again?"

"Not as much as before, I'm afraid. Still, given a little time, she might realize that you did this because you care so much about her."

"You think so?"

"It's possible."

This time my father hugged me, and he seemed to be both my mother and my father. I felt complete.

Chapter 22

Two weeks went by. They were easy to sum up. Alison didn't call. Matt, of course, didn't call. The cans were picked up by an earnest-looking man wearing overalls. I went back to my artwork. I called Opal three times. No answer. Now and then I looked at the picture of Matt in my closet.

The day of the Winklemans' lawn party arrived. It was a sunny Sunday. I got dressed up. I put on my yellow dress. It looked as good as new, thanks to Betty. She was a genius. I tied up my hair with a yellow ribbon, because it seemed to be right for a lawn party. It was kind of young and dumb, but still okay.

My father and I went to the party together. He had arranged to meet Gossamer there. Matt was driving her in from the city. I learned about these arrangements just a few days before the party. It didn't much matter. I had expected Gossamer and Matt to be there anyway. I was wondering how Tanya Lipsert would fit in. Maybe Matt had made a date to meet her at the party.

Mr. Winkleman greeted my father and me. He was a pointy-bearded man, refined and cordial, but he had a curled lip perpetually poised in a leer. It made him look like your friendly neighborhood pervert. He was the senior partner of the law firm. He had started it. He was a big shot. He had lots of unusual souvenirs and stuff in his house that hinted at connections to the rich and famous. My favorite was an autographed picture of Clark Gable that said "To Winky." Winky! I'm surprised Mr. Winkleman displayed it.

He gave out with a few welcoming remarks that fell just short of schmaltz. He was every inch the host. Mr. Winkleman as representative of his lawn party was harder to take than Mr. Winkleman the senior law partner. Mrs. Winkleman came up and stood beside him. She didn't match Mr. Winkleman, and when they stood side-by-side it looked as if one of them were a mistake. Mrs. Winkleman always wore low-cut dresses to her lawn parties, and when you looked at her, you stared down her dress. You didn't want to. Your eyes just went there.

I raised my eyes and looked over her shoulder. I saw Matt and Gossamer standing together. Gossamer came over, said hello to me, and walked off with my father. Matt stood at a distance, gazing at me. Then he walked up to me.

"Hi," he said. "Isn't this a great party."

"Sure is."

I wondered where Tanya Lipsert was. Matt looked kind of wonderfully alone. It couldn't last.

"How are things at the office?" I asked.

I sounded like a wife!

"I like the work very much."

"Any more funny stories?"

Matt laughed, remembering the lady who had gone after Mr. Winkleman. "You remember that story?"

"Sure. I remember the whole lunch."

Matt had got more handsome, it seemed to me. He was wearing a pale yellow shirt. We were both dressed in yellow. Did we make a nice-looking couple? Did we make a couple? Of course not. In a moment he would probably excuse himself and wander off to mix with the other guests.

"Let's get some food," he said, as if we were together.

We walked over to one of the long tables. You could always count on the Winklemans for a fantastic spread. All the food was so beautifully presented that no one wanted to be the first to stick a spoon or fork into something and disfigure it. Mrs. Winkleman was making the rounds of the tables, urging guests to "Eat, eat." Matt and I took plates, silverware, and napkins from the end of the table. Then we walked around the table, making our selections. I was the first to massacre a gelatin mold. I didn't want to look like a pig so I took less food than I would have if I had been alone.

Gossamer and my father came over and said, "Family reunion," at the same time. Suddenly that didn't sound like such a bad idea, Gossamer and my father, Matt and me together. Matt would be in my life if my father and

Gossamer got married. But that's not the way I wanted Matt, as a forced relative.

The party was getting bigger and more colorful. People were all over the lawn in kind of classic poses of sociability. Sitting, standing, leaning, talking, laughing, eating, drinking, and staring at everybody else. At a distance I saw Tanya. She was with her parents. She was looking our way. I shifted slightly so that my back was to her.

The four of us went hunting for seats. Folding chairs were set up around small round tables. We couldn't find four empty seats together, so Gossamer and my father wandered off to sit with friends. Matt and I sat down on the ground next to a hedge. Memories of my yellow dress and sitting and eating on the ground came back to me. But if I got a grass stain now, I would make sure that Betty didn't wash it off.

I didn't know what to talk about. I wished Opal were there. She had set the wheels in motion. She had told me to go to New York and see Matt. She had given me a push when I needed one. Opal, my mother-adviser. That's what she had been. But now I was on my own.

One thing I knew. I was seeing Matt because I ran into him once again. Via my father, of course. It was the same old pattern repeating itself. Maybe Betty *could* wash off the dress.

"I called you," Matt said between bites of food.

"What?"

"I called you."

"When?"

"A couple of weeks or so after we went to the movies. You weren't home. I guess it was Betty who answered. I told her I'd call back."

"So you were the one!"

"Yes. I didn't call back right away. It must have been a week later. There wasn't any answer. Telephones eventually get answered, so I should have called again. But the momentum was gone."

"What do you mean?"

Matt shifted his position. It was getting uncomfortable sitting on the ground. "I guess it goes back to your breaking that date," he said. "I *was* a little turned off when you broke it. I suppose it was pride. And all of your excuses seemed to make it worse. But when I saw you at your house, I felt that you really wanted to go out with me. And we had a wonderful time, boring movie and all, didn't we?" Matt didn't wait for me to answer him. "I had never enjoyed a date so much. That is, *being* with someone. But at the end you were put off by something I said, so I decided to let the whole thing cool for a while."

"And then you called me?"

"Yes."

"Ah, the missing piece!"

"What?" Matt gave me a strange look.

How could I tell him that a phone call was what had been missing from our relationship? The conscious act of calling me up and not simply running into me. There was also the irony of his having called me twice and my having called him twice. I decided to skip telling him about that bit of irony.

I changed the subject, but only slightly. Tanya was still looking at us. What about Tanya? "Tanya's watching us," I said. "Were you supposed to meet her here?"

"No." Matt gave me another strange look.

"Haven't you been going out with her?"

"Where did you get an idea like *that?*"

"I think I got it from Tanya."

"Then she gave you the wrong idea. I *am* in love with a Lipsert woman. But it's her mother."

"So am I. Isn't she the greatest?"

"Absolutely." Matt shifted again. "I was planning to meet *you* here, actually. I knew you were coming. That's why I didn't phone you a third time. I would have psyched myself up for a third call, but I didn't have to. In person is better, isn't it?"

"Well, there's something to be said for phone calls too."

"When I heard about the lawn party, I thought, Here's another chance. Is this my chance?"

"To do what?"

"Ask you out again. Want to go to another possibly boring movie when the party's over?"

"I'd love to. But what about your mother? Aren't you supposed to drive her back to the city?"

"I told her I was going to ask you out. She said if you said yes, she'd go out with your father and we could arrange to meet later for the drive back. She was all in favor of my asking you out, by the way."

"She *was*?"

"She's fond of you."

"Why? If I were your mother, I wouldn't be fond of me. Our vibes are off."

"Well, she expected some hostility because of her relationship with your father. Subtracting the hostility she expected, she ended up with a good feeling about you."

I picked some food off my dress. "How do *you* feel about their relationship now?"

"I've accepted it. If she wants to get together again with my father, that's totally up to her. If not, well, I can think of worse families for her to marry into."

Matt took my hand and held it for a long time. Then we got up and walked around, holding hands. This clearly was the very best lawn party the Winklemans had ever thrown. Superior, that's what it was. But I was greedy. I wanted one more success. I wanted Tanya Lipsert still to be watching Matt and me. But she was looking down Mrs. Winkleman's dress.

Chapter 23

I walked over to Opal's apartment the day after the party. I rang the bell. No answer. I rang the bell at the apartment next door to Opal's. A woman opened the door a crack. There was a chain on it.

"Yes?"

"I'm a friend of your next-door neighbor, Opal Spiegel. Do you know where she is?"

"I think she's away, or gone."

"Is she coming back?"

"I don't know. I don't ask. Sorry."

The woman closed the door.

I tried the super's apartment, but there wasn't any answer.

I started to walk home. I felt a little melancholy. It was unfair that I should feel this way. I was happy about Matt. Our movie date had turned out terrific, and he had asked me out for the next Saturday night. Couldn't I just enjoy all of that without worrying about Opal? I couldn't. Opal counted too. She was somebody of value, and she seemed to have disappeared.

I was two houses away from my house when Betty came running up to me waving something. "My prayers," she was yelling, "my prayers were heard. Your mother's coming home!"

When Betty reached me she thrust a card in my face. There was a pretty picture of mountains on it. "It's from Switzerland," she said, "and listen to this. Here goes. Oh, I'm too excited. You read it."

She handed me the card. I read, "Gerald and Jody dears, you will be happy to know that I found myself. It was a long search. You will understand when I come home. Expect me in early September. Love always, Sue."

Betty was jumping up and down. I had never seen anyone her age do that. She had forgotten about Timmy, who had followed her out of the house. He was coming along, kicking pebbles.

I felt weak. My mother coming home! After two years. It was bewildering, confusing, complicated. I wanted to see her badly. But what would this do to my father? He had his life planned with Gossamer. It wasn't right that my mother should mess up his life again.

"I'll tell my father when he comes home tonight," I said. "Don't say anything if he phones. Let me break the news."

"You really watch over your father, don't you," said Betty.

"We watch over each other," I said.

"He'll get rid of that Gossamer lady now," said Betty.

Betty had never remarked about Gossamer one way or

the other. She was a loyal employee of my father's. Now she was switching loyalties. My mother would be back, and Betty would pledge allegiance to my mother.

"Don't pray for my father to get rid of Gossamer," I said. "It might be the wrong thing to pray for."

The event of Gossamer Green and the fact that my father actually liked her had forced me to respect his needs. He had as much right to have a Gossamer as Alison did to have a Pete. I changed the subject before Betty could preach to me. "Any calls?"

"Just Alison."

"What do you mean, *just* Alison. I would kill for a call from Alison. What did she say?"

"She said not to call her back. She'll call you again next week. She says she's slowly testing how it feels to talk to you again, and she has to do it her way."

"That's a relief. We'll be friends again. It'll work out."

"Is she angry at you?"

"Yeah, I did something unforgivable."

Betty was all ears, but I didn't give her any more information. I could tell she was feeling left out. She wanted to celebrate my mother's return. She wanted to talk about it, and clean for it, and fill the pores of the house with it.

I went into my house and up to my room. I looked at the calendar on my desk. September, and my mother, were almost here.

My mind refused to make room for all the thoughts, emotions, expectations, and decisions that were tied to her return. I dropped to my bed and fell asleep. I woke up when the doorbell rang.

Betty came to my room. She was holding a letter and pen. "Express Mail," she said. "Everybody's thinking of you today. Here's the place where you sign."

I was groggy. I signed my name, and Betty took the signed slip downstairs, leaving me with the letter. As she left she said, "Somebody must think you're a VIP." I looked at the envelope. According to the return address, the letter was from someone named Stamp in Montana. I tore open the envelope and read the letter.

> Dear Jody,
>
> I eloped with Carl Stamp. He's the gentleman who called for me at your house. Remember when I wrote that there's no such thing as the right decision? I still believe it. But I also believe in love. Once in Scarsdale and once in Spain I believed in it. And now in Montana. That's where we're living. I don't think it's my kind of state. But we will not be returning to New York. If I never see you again, think of me whenever your doorbell rings, and sometimes when it doesn't. Have an interesting life, dear Jody Kline. You deserve it, in spades.
>
> Your friend,
> Opal O'Malley Spiegel Stamp

Opal, my friend Opal, had gone off to a new experience. She was Mrs. Stamp of Montana. It probably wouldn't change her one bit. But, given the right circumstances and a little luck, Opal could probably change Montana. I got out my sketchbook and started to draw a picture of her. I would send it as a little present. As her face formed, I gave it a happy expression. I hoped it reflected how she looked right now. I worked on the picture for a while and then put it away in my closet until the next session.

The telephone rang. What now? I didn't need any more news. Two shockers in one day were enough. My mother was coming home. Opal had married and moved to Montana. Everybody else I knew was in place. I hoped.

I picked up the receiver. "Hello."

"Jody, it's Matt."

Matt! I had seen him just last night. Why was he calling? "I hope you don't have incredible news," I said.

"I'd like to take you out to dinner tonight. Is that incredible?"

"Maybe. I just saw you last night."

"I miss you."

"You do?"

"Very much."

This was the kind of incredible news I wanted, needed. But I had to think of my father. "What about my father? I'm supposed to eat with him."

"He's working late."

Late. I guess the news about my mother could wait a little longer.

"Dinner sounds wonderful."

"Good. I'll be there at six thirty. Okay?"

"Six thirty? That gives me only three hours to get ready."

"You need three hours to get ready?"

"This time I do."

"If you say so. See you at six thirty."

"See you at six thirty."

I hung up and walked to my room. I felt like running. Matt missed me! *Very much*. No more would I call Clarice's Clip Joint by mistake. No more would I hang around a kitchen making spice cake that tasted like gingerbread. I opened my closet and took out the picture of Matt with the folds through it. If I worked fast I could do a new one in less than three hours.

In three hours Matt Green would be standing at my door just as he had the first day of my summer vacation. I would hand him his picture. Face to face. This, I could finally admit to myself, was exactly what I had always wanted.

Opal O'Malley Spiegel Stamp, there *is* such a thing as the right decision.